Promised Beauty

Books by Christine Marshall
With illustrations by Steve Marshall

Becoming Cinder
White As Snow
Forever Sleeping
Promised Beauty
Final Lock
Little Flower

RISE of the GIANTS
BATTLE of the GIANTS
LAST of the GIANTS

The Last Mapmaker

A Series of Intentional Disasters

Volume 1, Volume 2, Volume 3

NOBLESTONE and the Lost Dwarves
NOBLESTONE and the Secret Forge

Illustrated Guides:
Dragons and Flying Creatures
Folk Creatures
Unexpected Creatures
Insects and Mechanical Things

Promised Beauty

A retelling

Christine Marshall

Sign up for Christine's e-newsletter!

Check out Christine's website!
www.ChristineMarshallAuthor.com

Cover and chapter art by Steve Marshall
No part of this book was created using generative AI.

This book is dedicated to

my amazing friend

Sumedha.

Thank you for your kindness and love. I'm so glad
we met in the ballet class parents waiting room all
those years ago! You were my inspiration for Indira.
I hope you love her!

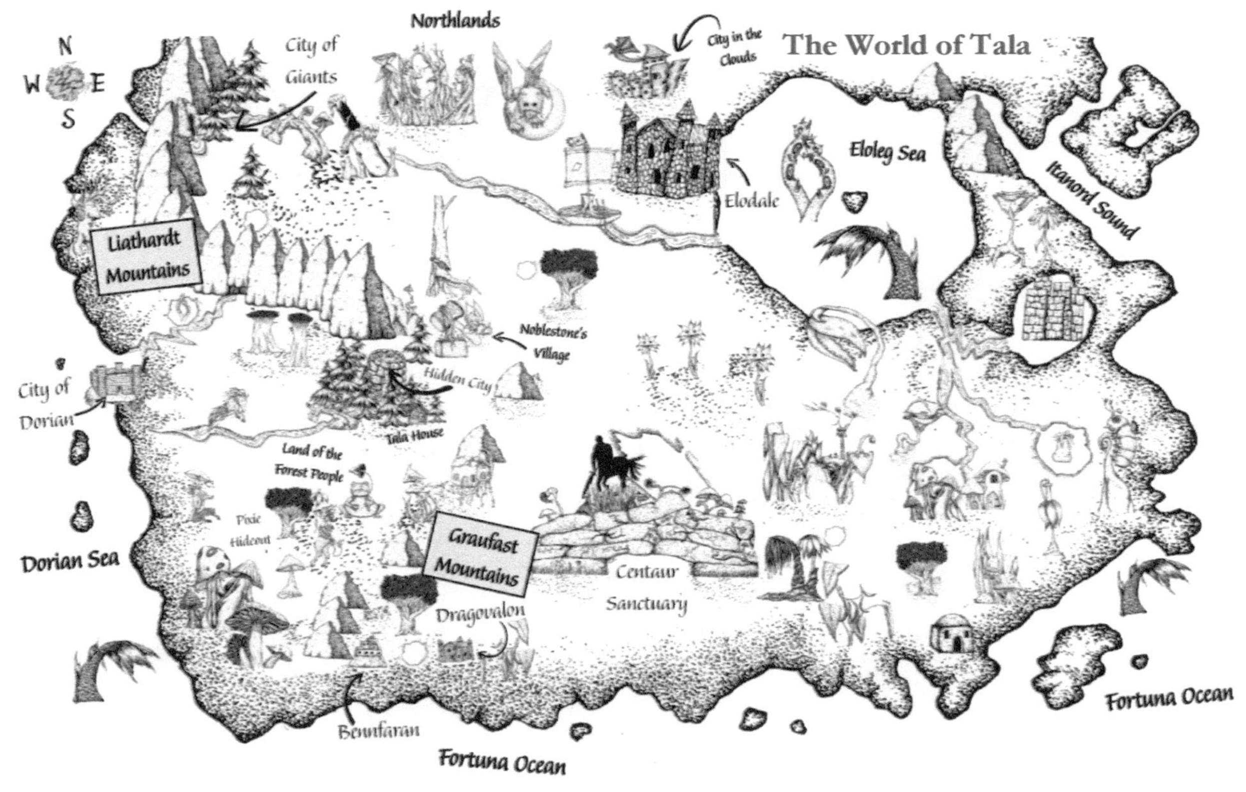

Learn more about **Tala** at the back of the book!

One

"Indi! Indi!" A handful of young voices and light feet approached from behind Indira.

Half a dozen sets of brown eyes against tan faces, framed by curtains of nearly black hair, smiled up at her as they scurried to catch up. Some of the children bounced on the balls of their feet. One little girl tugged on Indira's plain cotton apron.

"I don't have anything to spare today, children," Indira said in a sympathetic voice. She squatted so she could be at eye level with them.

The small girl climbed awkwardly into Indira's not-quite lap. She adjusted her posture to keep her balance.

Indira sighed. She really didn't have any food to spare that day. Her parents, brothers, and sisters were waiting for her to return from the market with the scant supply they could afford for themselves.

Lately, no one could afford much food. The prices were high. The supply slim. Many in their village had gaunt faces and sunken eyes. Adults deferred their meals to the children as much as possible.

But these little ones didn't have adults to provide for them. Their parents had perished before the drought and the oldest boy took care of his younger siblings on his own. They relied on the generosity of others. And Indira's family had once been their biggest benefactor.

The drought that had touched their lands had ruined Indira's family fortune. Along with most of the other families in her village.

Indira's heart couldn't take the sad eyes, though. She set the little girl on the dusty ground and flipped her own long, black braid over her shoulder. A puff of air from Indira's lips blew the fringe on her forehead out of her eyes. She pulled her canvas bag from inside her basket and reached inside and removed a packet of amaranth sprouts.

"They were fertilized with dragon scales. I had planned to plant these, but they are edible now, too." She slipped the packet to one of the tall boys in the back of the crowd. "If you decide to grow them, the flowers never wither and are full of life-giving potential. They would sustain all of you for a very long time." She spoke in a low voice. She didn't want the children to worry.

The boy nodded his understanding. He must have been familiar with the magical properties of the amaranth blossoms. But his worried eyes testified that he and his siblings were also very hungry now.

"Do whatever will be best for your family…" Indira looked around the village. No one paid them any attention. "And… don't tell anyone I shared these with you," she said in a low voice to the children.

The oldest boy gave her a solemn nod and used his finger to draw an "X" over his heart.

It's not like she would get in trouble necessarily, but her mother did expect her to return with the enchanted sprouts. Indira had traded a small jar of their scant pixie-honey supply for them. Her mother would be disappointed, but these children needed the sprouts more than her family did.

Indira ruffled the hair of two of the little boys and hugged the girls tightly. "Take care. Do you have water?"

The tall boy nodded once. "Yes."

"Good. Stay out of the sun." Indira stood and pushed her basket up her arm to rest in the crook of her elbow.

The children scurried back to the shadows between

the low stucco buildings. If only she could have done more for them. But wishes only ended in heartache.

She lifted her chin and continued her swift strides toward home.

Indira's family had built their home beyond the village borders and into the rolling hills. Hills that had once been covered in swaying green grass, home to an entire colony of antlered thistlehares, and had been frequently visited by a herd of large deer-like creatures with horns made of gold.

Now the grass was dry and brittle beneath Indira's feet. The crunch of the stems breaking combined with the dust that billowed every time her foot hit the ground. The absence of the usual creatures only added to the desolate atmosphere.

It had been too long since it had rained. The river was all but dried up. They might as well have been living in a desert, for which no one was prepared. Least of all her own family.

Her father ran a shipping business on the once fast-flowing river. When the rains stopped his business had dried up along with the water. If it wasn't for his foolish but well-meaning pride, they would be accepting aid from others as well, instead of barely scraping by on their own.

"Indira!" Another voice called her name. She knew that male voice. "Wait! Let me help you carry your things!"

She quickened her pace and swiped the sweat from her brow. "I'm fine, Kian. I don't need help." There was barely enough food in her basket to make it heavy. She only struggled because of the loose ground and beating sun. Hopefully her clumsy feet wouldn't betray her words. The last thing she needed right now was to stumble on a stone. That would only further Kian's desire to help her.

Kian, of course, didn't listen. His quick breath caught in her ear as he fell into step beside her. Most of the young women of the village, her younger sisters included, found Kian wildly attractive. And his appearance was, she supposed. Thick dark hair, messy on his head. Matching heavy eyebrows over long-lashed light brown eyes. A wide smile that produced a dimple on one side of his face and showed off his perfect teeth. It wasn't his appearance that Indira didn't appreciate, though. It was his personality. She found that true beauty came from within, and Kian… didn't have much.

"Let me carry your basket," Kian insisted. He reached for the handle.

Indira swatted his hand away. "I already told you; I don't need help. I'm nearly home and the basket is nearly empty."

"I do wish you would allow my father to offer his assistance." Kian's clear voice echoed around the hillside. He walked backwards in front of her so that he could see her as he spoke. He flashed his charming smile at her that should make her heart skip but only forced her to suppress an eyeroll.

Indira choked on her scoff. "If only it was that simple," she murmured under her breath.

"Pardon?" Kian leaned closer to her.

She sidestepped around him. "Your father does not offer assistance out of generosity. He only wishes to absorb my father's business into his own so he can be the most profitable merchant as far as the shadows stretch. We're not interested." Indira kept her voice firm.

Kian stopped suddenly. She took the chance to widen the gap between them and quickened her steps until she was practically running up the hill.

Please, feet, don't trip me now. She pleaded with herself to stay upright.

In several quick movements Kian joined her once more. "It's not like that," he insisted.

He tried to take her hand.

She squirmed away from his touch.

Kian didn't notice. "He would assist because of my feelings for you, Indira. No strings attached. Marry me and you will see. He has no ulterior motives." His voice was pleading.

It was Indira's turn to stop.

Kian tripped on his own feet and stood in front of her, a look of hope shining in his dark eyes.

She inwardly grinned at his stumble, so relieved it hadn't been her!

His smile widened. He reached for her hand once more.

Any trace of a smile disappeared from her lips. Apparently, it hadn't been as inward a grin as she had thought. As usual, she wore her emotions on her sleeve. If only Kian would pay attention to the ones that proved she *didn't* want his attention. He seemed to only notice those he thought were in his favor.

The space between them closed with a quick step forward by Kian. Indira stiffened. The last thing she needed was for him to try to embrace her. Or worse, plant a kiss on her lips.

Her stomach twisted, but she stayed perfectly still.

A match between herself and Kian would certainly be beneficial for her family. But she didn't think his father was so innocent in his desires. Neither was Kian. He had proposed to several other girls in the village from influential families. And each of the girls had been left behind when his attentions locked onto someone new. Kian would not be faithful to her any more than he had to the others.

Besides, Indira didn't know what she wanted out of life yet. She was only seventeen. She wasn't ready to wed at all, let alone with someone she didn't like. She had dreams of captaining one of her father's ships and sailing the sea. She couldn't very well do that if she was stuck in this village as Kian's little wife.

"Kian, I…" How was she supposed to reject him politely? *Again?* He didn't seem to take her refusal to heart, anyway. She was terrible at expressing her thoughts with words.

Before she could tell him anything about what she thought of marrying him, a loud deep rumble came from the sky. She felt the rumble deep in her chest. It left her feeling unsettled. But hopeful at the same time.

Indira's eyes shot upward. Clouds formed overhead and light flashed behind them. Could they be so lucky? Had the drought finally ended? She couldn't take her eyes off the sky as she waited for the first blessed raindrops to hit her expectant face.

From the corner of her eye, she saw that Kian couldn't take his eyes off *her*.

Figures. He didn't need the rain like the rest of them. She squirmed beneath his gaze but held her breath and waited for the sky to break open and give the land, and her people, the water they so desperately needed.

Two

An unnatural screech from the sky drowned out every other sound around her. It was as if the sky had been torn apart above her head.

Indira startled and stepped away from Kian. Her heart pounded.

More lightning flashed in the broiling dark clouds. A shadow spread across the monotone pale landscape of lifelessness, dimming the light to an ominous level for the middle of the day.

Another cry pierced the air. Indira dropped her basket and clapped her hands over her ears. Her wide eyes stayed glued to the sky.

Kian jumped beside her.

Then he bent to pick up her things in a hurry. He gripped the handles with white knuckles when he stood.

Before either of them could speak to the other, another cry from the sky penetrated to her bones.

A cold sweat engulfed Indira. She gasped. "Kian! We have to run!"

He gaped at her and shook his head. "Why? What's a little rain…"

"It's not going to rain. It's a thunderbird!"

Indira didn't wait for Kian to understand. She grabbed her basket from Kian's hands and took off up the hill for home. So much for being polite. She scolded herself but didn't slow her pace.

She kept one eye to the sky, scanning for any sign of the source of the storm. "Why couldn't it have been a real thunderstorm?"

Kian caught up to her a moment later. He grabbed her hand and pulled her along at a faster pace.

She couldn't keep her balance and watch her steps with him tugging on her arm. She tripped over her own feet and fell to her knees. A sharp stone pierced her skin on one knee through her clothes. But she didn't dare take her eyes off the sky. They would not be safe until they found shelter.

The thunderbird emerged from the storm it had created.

Kian pulled Indira to her feet and dragged her up the hill toward her home.

The bird swooped in wide circles above. Lightning danced on its massive wings. Were they about to become supper for the enormous creature?

Indira covered her ears again in anticipation of its fearsome cry, just in time.

This time, when the bird yelled at the world, it released a volley of lightning strikes from its midnight black wings. The streams of blinding light struck out in every direction from both of its wings.

Kian screamed. Indira didn't have time to ponder the high pitch of his shocked noise. She instinctively ducked, as if that would save her from being struck by the bird's magical lightning.

The strikes hit the ground in a wide circle nearly simultaneously. Other villagers in the village below that had been in the path of the lightning shouted and ran for cover. The whole village was in a panic! People ran in all directions, either trying to hide or flee from the massive bird with a wingspan nearly as large as the village itself.

"Come on," Kian growled in her ear. He yanked on her arm and dragged her away from the village.

The bird circled again, away from Indira and Kian and toward the shouts from the village below.

Indira's heart jumped into her throat. "Oh, no…" Indira whispered. She stumbled along behind Kian but didn't take her eyes off the bird and her village. She held her breath and waited for the worst.

But the bird did not loose another round of

lightning.

Instead, it swooped low and skimmed the rooftops. Deep gashes scarred the tiled roofs from its large talons.

It produced the reaction that the bird seemed to have expected. People ran out of the buildings and scurried to find different shelter.

Indira froze in her tracks. She couldn't take her eyes off the scene. Her stomach clenched and her throat tightened. Her basket slid from her arm and landed with a thud on the ground.

"Indira!" Kian shouted over his shoulder as he fled. He didn't wait for her to catch up as he disappeared over the top of the hillside.

The bird rose in the air, circled again, and dove with its talons extended. It had spotted its prey. It swooped low and snatched the last milking cow from the dried-up pasture into its enormous talons. It let out another ear-piercing screech and beat its wings in a slow and steady rhythm. The cow let out its own horrified cry, but there was nothing to be done.

Indira, along with everyone else down below, watched as the bird carried the cow away from them.

With the exit of the bird, the clouds dissolved, and the sun beat down on the village again.

Indira sighed. It was a terrible tragedy about the cow, but at least all the people were safe. More screams reached her ears from the village below.

"Fire!" People yelled in panicky voices.

Smoke billowed from the dwindling, dry hay bales in the corner of the now empty pasture.

"Oh, no!" Indira's feet carried her toward the cries.

The fire started by a thunderbird could be nearly impossible to douse.

"Feet, don't fail me now." She half-ran-half-slid back down the hill and toward the pasture.

Men and women scattered to their homes to fetch any source of liquid they could find to douse the flames. Others shuttled children away from the danger. Still more stood in a stupor and watched the flames grow.

Before anyone could return with a sufficient amount of water to even think about putting out the fire, the flames devoured the hay and lit the dry pasture grass on fire.

"Quick!" one of the men shouted. "We need to evacuate the surrounding area! There's no way we'll put this out!"

Indira didn't hesitate. She gathered those who had frozen with fear and pulled them away from the pasture.

The owner of the pasture shouted above the panicked voices of the people. "We must create a fire barrier, so it doesn't spread to the entire village!"

Those who weren't in a stupor helped douse the edge of the farmer's land with the water. Indira helped as they hastily dug a wide, shallow trench to try to make a fire stop.

When they were finished, all they could do was watch. The fire lapped up the field and spread into the surrounding grasslands all the way to the horizon. Normally the valley was lush, but the dead trees, shrubs, and grass disintegrated into ash as the fire spread.

The firestop they had created worked. The flames that tried to cross it were easily doused with buckets of water from the line of villagers that had joined the edge of the village.

The sky above the valley filled with smoke. The air was thick. The sun turned an eerie shade of orange. But the village was safe. The fire burned itself out when there was no fuel left.

The charred land smoldered for the rest of the day. The landscape looked even more depressing than before.

Indira finally made her way home. She picked up her forgotten basket, the handle now broken, on her way up the hill. Ash smudged her face. Soot spotted her clothes. Smoke itched her throat. Her hair was a disheveled mess.

She couldn't help but think, "I wonder if Kian will still want to marry me now?"

When she pushed the door open to her family's house on the hillside, she fully expected him to be there with her family. A quick glance proved her to be wrong. He must have hidden and then fled when the threat of the bird had been gone. She hadn't seen him help out below, though, so he had returned to the safety of his own home.

When Indira's mother entered the room from the kitchen, she reacted to Indira's appearance with shock.

"What has happened to you?" She rushed over and ran her hands over Indira's head, face, and arms.

"I'm fine, mother. I just helped put out the fire…"

"What's this about a fire?" her father asked as he joined them in the sparsely furnished front room.

Indira looked back and forth between her parents. Had they not heard the shouting from the village? Had they been totally unaware of the disaster that nearly reached their door? She told them what happened below.

"*What?*" Her mother's hand flew to her heart. "Oh no! Is everyone safe?"

"The cow is gone. The landscape is ruined. But the villagers, and the village, are safe."

Her father furrowed his brow. "Another setback to add to the already long list. Without the cow, there will be no access to dairy products. The fields were already not producing…" His voice trailed off and he wandered back to his study.

Indira followed. "What are we to do, father?" Her voice was edged with desperation.

He rubbed his stubbly face, and his eyes were out of focus. She knew he was trying to solve the problem. Somehow.

Their family had already gone to great lengths to

weather the drought. They rationed water for drinking and for watering their meager garden. Their dishes and clothes, and bodies, no longer received regular washings.

The garden did not grow well, but with the help of their diminishing supply of ground dragon scales, it produced a little.

One of her brothers kept a pixie hive, but without flowers to visit, the bee-sized pixies had stopped producing honey. Indira's family used tiny bottles of their pixie-honey from their constantly diminishing storage supply to trade for things they needed.

Indira, and her siblings that were old enough, cleaned houses and stables in exchange for small portions of food. Until there were no animals left in the stables and the people could no longer afford the hired help in their homes.

Those in the family who could use a needle mended clothing. They assisted with childcare and helped tutor children.

But all these side jobs had gradually run out. Now their pixie-honey was their only trading source. Besides the few things they acquired at market, Indira and her siblings foraged for edible food or animals before the sun beat down on them in the afternoons and forced them home.

Her parents were hungry. Indira herself deferred portions of her meals to her younger siblings. Only the youngest at four years old drank milk, but now that the cow was gone, she would no longer have that option anymore.

After a long pause, her father sighed. His shoulders slumped. "I do not know, Indira. We can barely manage to feed our own family, let alone continue to help those less fortunate."

Indira sighed. She rubbed the ache in her forehead. She stood at the window and looked down across the valley.

Their village had been a bustling stop on the river trade route that stretched from the lands far to the east all the way to the western sea. The land had provided plenty for the people to consume themselves with a large surplus to sell to merchants and travelers on the riverfront. Her father's good relations with the river nixies had allowed his business to thrive. The people of her village had all benefited from the increase in visitors to their town.

The drought had turned the landscape brown. And now the fire had turned all the brown into ashy gray. Their whole village and the fields beyond were suddenly devoid of color altogether. It was like the land didn't want them anymore.

Would they have to leave? What would her family do to support themselves? What would any of the people in their village do to support themselves?

The only people who weathered this challenge were Kian's family. His father had stockpiled supplies over the years and had enough to keep themselves well-fed.

He used his surplus to buy out many of the other merchants in exchange for necessities. If this drought ever ended, he would come out the richest man along the entire river trade route.

He would readily do the same for their family. But her father had refused the buyout. Kian had offered another solution.

"Father, I do have one idea…" She rubbed her bare arms beneath the half-length sleeves of her long dress. She gripped the pale blue linen fabric and twisted it in her hands. Her heart raced. A knot formed in her stomach. Her throat tingled with nausea. "Kian has asked for my hand…"

"Indira!" Her father cut her off before she could continue. "No! It is plain on your face that you do not wish to accept. We will figure out another way."

"But, Papa." She used the name for him from when she was only knee high. "His family has the means to support us all. We will be secure from hunger and ruin…"

Her father loosely gripped her upper arms in his hands and leaned close to her face. "We will find another way." His eyes bore into hers. His words were final.

Indira tossed and turned in her bed. Her parents' voices carried from the adjoining room as they discussed various options from traveling to another land to sending her brothers away to earn wages, or even just food, for their family. She couldn't bear the thought of her family suffering when there was a simple option right in front of her face.

Literally. Kian would not stop bothering her until she accepted him.

She would have to push for a quick wedding so that he would not lose interest and turn his attention to someone else. So much for adventures on the sea. She would be stuck in this place before her life even really began.

She tossed and turned all night. Sweat soaked her lightweight nightgown. Her dreams were filled with images of marrying Kian. These were not the butterflies-in-your-stomach kind of dreams. These were dreams filled with dread and resignation about what her future would hold. She forced herself awake and lay in bed, staring at the ceiling. As much as she loathed the idea, she knew what she had to do.

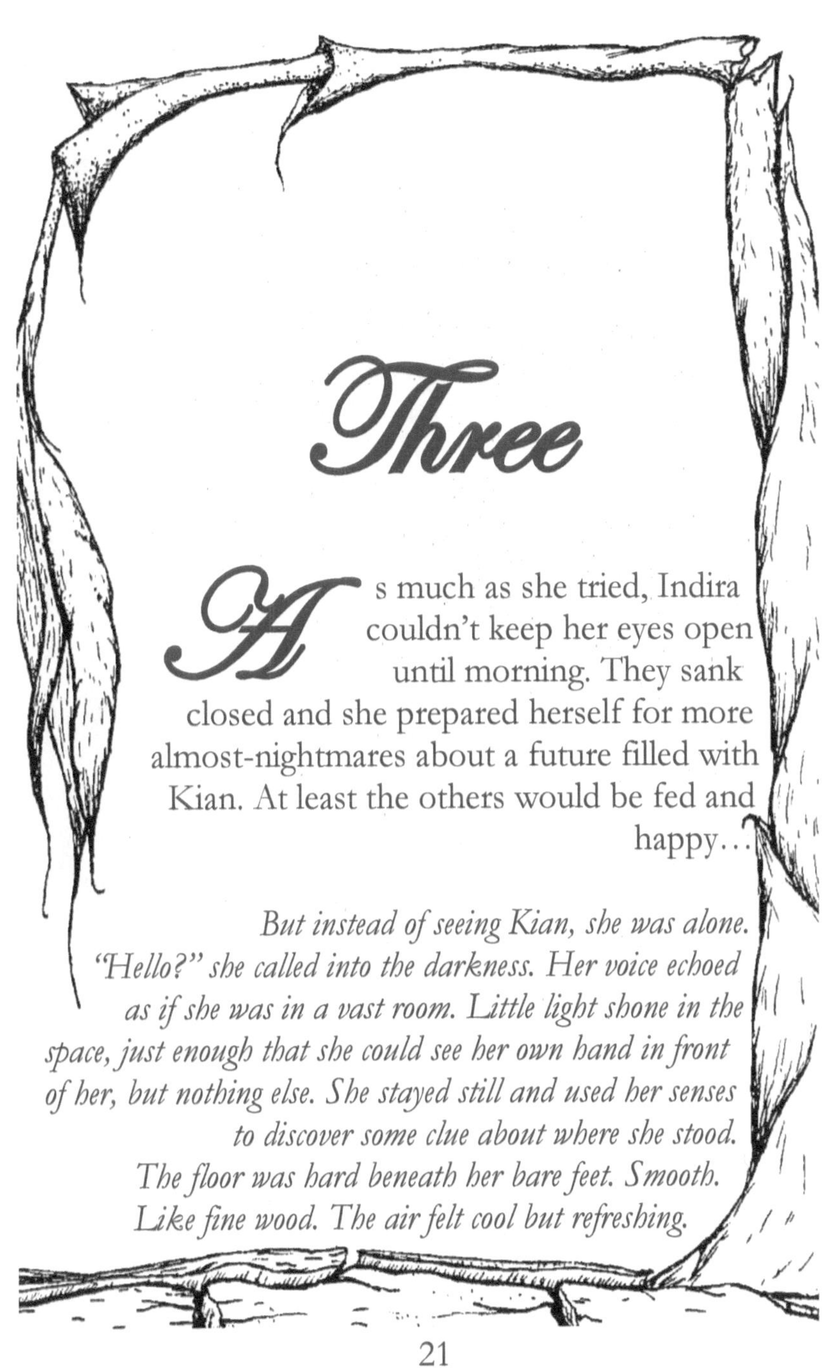

Three

As much as she tried, Indira couldn't keep her eyes open until morning. They sank closed and she prepared herself for more almost-nightmares about a future filled with Kian. At least the others would be fed and happy…

But instead of seeing Kian, she was alone. "Hello?" she called into the darkness. Her voice echoed as if she was in a vast room. Little light shone in the space, just enough that she could see her own hand in front of her, but nothing else. She stayed still and used her senses to discover some clue about where she stood. The floor was hard beneath her bare feet. Smooth. Like fine wood. The air felt cool but refreshing.

A sweet scent came from somewhere to her right. Like a garden or bouquet of fresh flowers. It had been a long time since she had smelled fresh flowers.

She turned toward the scent and took a tentative step forward.

"Hello?" she called again. Nothing.

She maneuvered carefully and quietly in a straight line. Or so she hoped. It was impossible to tell since it was so dark. No shadows or silhouettes indicated anything in the space besides herself.

She walked for what felt like hours, wondering if she would meet anyone or anything. Or maybe she would keep walking forever.

Maybe walking forever would be better than marrying Kian, though, she thought.

"Pull yourself together," she whispered out loud to herself. "It won't be that bad."

Her bare foot brushed against something soft on the ground. She paused and bent to the floor. Her fingers found a velvety oval. A rose petal. She held it to her nose and inhaled. It smelled divine!

Another step produced another petal. She followed the path of rose petals, at least having something to guide her now.

A silhouette finally took shape in front of her. She hurried her steps to discover what it was.

A low light from somewhere high above illuminated a small, round table that reached to her waist. A delicate glass rested exactly in the middle of the table.

When she arrived at the table to take a closer look, she saw that it wasn't a glass or a carafe as she had thought. It was a timekeeping glass. An hourglass.

She gently ran one finger down the smooth side, following the curve in and back out again.

Sand slipped through the narrow center. A few grains at a time. She leaned closer. Instead of seeing her own reflection in the glass, she could see her village. Right side up on the bottom, and a mirrored version of the same image where the glass curved. As the sand slid from the top to the bottom, the village changed. It faded away into nothing but dirt and ruins.

Indira gasped for air and sat up in her bed. She forced her heart to slow and her breathing to calm.

She expected the rose petal to be in her hand, but it had vanished with the dream.

Why had that hourglass shown her home and her people disappearing into nothing? Was it a warning of some kind? It had pricked a dark fear within her chest and startled her awake.

She tried to stay awake, but again, could not make her eyes stay open, even in her sitting position against the head of her bed.

She was right in front of the table. The rose petal back in between her fingers. The hourglass looked the same. But this time, just out of sight, another shadow loomed. A tall, bulky figure with massive antlers. It let out a sharp breath through its nostrils, like a threatened animal.

Indira froze. She squinted her eyes to try to get a better look at the figure. It slipped out of sight.

She slept the rest of the night with no more dreams of Kian or of the hourglass. Or the strange shadow in the darkness.

In the morning, she had a terrible kink in her neck, a pounding headache, and no idea what to do next.

"You're quiet this morning," Indira's mother placed a wooden bowl of rice porridge sweetened with the slightest drizzle of honey on the table in front of her.

Indira rubbed her puffy eyes and gave her mother a weak smile. "Just didn't sleep well."

When her mother had retrieved her own portion of the meager breakfast, she settled across from Indira at the long table made from a single slice of wood. Her father had traded for the opulent table on one of his voyages.

We spend enough time around the dinner table, we deserve to have the very finest that there is," he had told the family.

Indira and her mother sat in two of the matching chairs. The other seven chairs were empty. Her father already worked in his study, or more likely worried in his study, and her six siblings either slept or had gone out to try to forage for anything edible.

"Do you want to talk about it?" her mother asked about the dream, meeting her eyes.

Indira sighed. How could she explain to her mother what troubled her? Her mother would insist that the well-being of the family was not Indira's responsibility. She would tell her not to do anything she didn't want to do. Like marry Kian. Being the oldest of seven children had given Indira a feeling of responsibility toward the rest of them. She couldn't help it. And what about the dream? What would she even say to her mother about it? She didn't know what it meant, or how to describe the way it had made her feel.

"Just some bad dreams." She lowered her gaze and scooped some porridge into her mouth. If her mouth was full of food, then she couldn't answer her mother's questions.

Her mother rested her copper spoon in her own bowl. She propped her elbows on the smooth tabletop and folded her hands in front of her face. Her fingers pressed against her lips as she studied Indira.

Butterflies erupted in Indira's stomach. She should have snuck out of the house. Or stayed in bed and said she was sick. It wasn't far from the truth. Once her mother got that look in her eye, there was no way to escape. She was in for a lecture. Or pity. Or a scolding. Whatever it was, it was not going to be pleasant.

"I have a feeling it's more than just some 'bad dreams'." Her mother's calmness surprised Indira. Her mother could always tell when Indira was being less than truthful, but she didn't scold her this time. "If it really is dreams causing you so much heartache, then I suggest you seek out Mistress Mena."

Indira looked up to meet her mothers' eyes. Was she serious? Her mother wanted Indira to go talk to the oldest lady in their community? What would she be able to do to help Indira?

She didn't ask her mother any of these questions. She swallowed the nearly tasteless porridge, used a linen cloth to wipe the remaining moisture from the bowl, and placed it on the open kitchen shelf again. They didn't have enough water to wash the dishes anymore. They settled for dry cleaning them, instead.

"I'm serious, Indi. Go speak with Mistress Mena." Indira's mother wrapped her arms around her from behind.

"Yes, Mother," Indira said in a quiet voice. She would go because her mother told her to. And because her mother never offered frivolous advice.

Indira covered herself with a rough woolen cloak, more appropriate for winter weather than the dry heat that surrounded her now. But she didn't want to risk Kian spotting her and trying to tag along. If she was going to talk to Mistress Mena about her dreams, then she wanted to do it right away. She would put the conversation with Kian off until after her visit with the old woman. Who knew, maybe the woman would tell her something that would change her mind about Kian. One way or another.

She kept to the shadows and maneuvered through the dry, brown, lifeless village until she arrived at the woman's small home near the center. She knocked lightly on the door and cast furtive eyes around her just in case Kian rounded the corner.

A frail voice called from behind the door. "Come in, Indi!"

Indira startled. How did the woman know it was her?

She couldn't stay out here, unnoticed, much longer. She pushed the door open with a slight creak and slipped through, gently closing the door behind her with a soft click. She leaned her back against the door, palms flat, and waited.

"Come in, child. Don't be shy. I wondered when you might make your way into my home." Mistress Mena sat in a small rocking chair near the window in the opposite wall. Natural light illuminated her from behind and gave her a mysterious glow. A light, handwoven lap blanket of various shades of blue covered her from the waist down. The rocker swayed gently forward and back.

It had been a while since Indira had visited Mistress Mena. She remembered her salt-and-pepper hair and kind brown eyes from her childhood. But the woman had more wrinkles around her eyes and mouth than before. And she bent at the shoulders a bit more, too.

A wrinkled hand reached toward Indira and waved her forward. The woman gestured at a chair beside her, angled so they could speak comfortably. She wore a bright smile on her face. Her eyes, though wrinkled around the corners, made Indira think of a much younger woman. They were wise and sharp, as if she could see things that others could not.

Indira padded across the rug-covered floor and lowered herself into the adjacent cushioned chair.

"Take the cloak off. You don't need to hide in here." Mistress Mena waved her hands around.

Indira sat speechless.

"Go on!" the Mistress encouraged.

Indira slipped the hood from her head and untied the chord at her throat. The cloak slipped off her shoulders and bunched up behind her on the chair.

"Relax, my dear." Mistress Mena rested one of her crepey hands on Indira's own hand that gripped the arm of the chair. The woman's skin was cool and soft, and Indira instantly felt more comfortable.

"Thank you." She swallowed the lump in her throat. Why did she suddenly feel like she wanted to cry?

A miniature person with long, pointed ears entered the room. In her arms she balanced a tray that held a small pot and two dainty teacups. Indira had forgotten that Mistress Mena had a brownie that liked to serve her in exchange for sweet treats. No one else in the village had such a companion. Indira tried not to stare.

The sweet scent of cold fairyberry tea reached Indira's nose and her mouth instantly watered. She knew better than to thank the brownie for the tea and avoided eye contact with the creature.

After Mistress Mena's friend had left the room, the old woman spoke. "Tell me about your dream, Indi." Mistress Mena rested her teacup on the small table beside her chair and folded her hands back into her lap.

"Pardon me for asking, Mistress Mena. But…how… how did you know?" Indira gazed at Mistress Mena with a curious expression.

The old woman chuckled lightly. "Oh, Indi, please, call me Mena. None of this 'Mistress' stuff in here."

Indira raised her eyebrows. They were taught to always respect their elders. Which was more respectful? To call her "Mistress" against her wishes? Or to do away with the title at her request?

The woman interrupted Indira's thoughts. "I've been watching you for some time. You have a bright future, Indira. Please, tell me the dream that troubled you."

She didn't actually answer Indira's question about how she knew. But Indira didn't know if she cared right now. She felt comfortable in the woman's presence and desperately needed answers. If this woman could provide them, it didn't matter how.

"It was dark. There was this hourglass. It showed…" Indira's voice trailed off.

Mistress Mena… no, just Mena… nodded and closed her eyes. She made a humming sound as if she knew of what Indira spoke. "Was there anything else?" she looked at Indira expectantly.

"There was… a figure. Just a shadow of a shape. Large. Inhuman." Indira's voice trembled. Her hands shook. She gripped the arms of the chair tighter.

"Fascinating," Mena murmured to herself. "What

about your other senses?"

Indira met her eyes again. She had a knowing look on her face. "I smelled flowers. That's it."

"I am going to summarize what you have told me. An hourglass showing the village dying…"

Indira hadn't thought of it like that. But yes, it did show the village dying. But she hadn't shared that detail with Mena, had she?

"… the scent of roses,"

Indira had said flowers. She hadn't mentioned the rose petal.

"…and a beast in shadow."

Indira didn't know if she would necessarily call the shadow a beast. But she wouldn't know what other word to use, either.

"Yes," she said.

"Very good. I know what must be done." Mena stood with great effort from her chair.

Indira offered her a hand, but the old woman waved her away. Indira sunk back into her chair.

Mena shuffled to a tall bookshelf on the adjacent wall and ran her finger down the spines of the books. When she found the one for which she searched, she slid it from the shelf. It weighed her arms down as if it was heavier than it looked.

She returned to her rocking chair and rested the book in her lap. Her hands blocked the cover from Indira's view.

"I am going to share a legend with you that I believe

to be truth. Take it at face value and it could be the answer to everything. Have a heart of doubt, and the trouble you saw in the hourglass will become a reality." Her words were slow and steady.

Indira gulped. That sounded… ominous. But she trusted this woman, somehow, and would do as she said.

"I am ready."

Four

The cadence of Mena's voice resembled music, but not quite. She didn't sing, exactly, but her words ebbed and flowed in such a way that Indira found herself solely focused on them. She was so enchanted by the story that she almost saw everything before her.

"Long ago a curse was placed upon the mountain far to the north. The air became frigid. The landscape covered in thick layers of snow and ice."

Indira had always wanted to see snow. She had heard tales and could kind of imagine what it might look like to be in a place covered completely by the white, icy crystals.

Mena continued. "The first man to intrude upon this wintery landscape became ensnared by the enchantment. His human form changed to that of a terrible beast."

Indira saw the strange silhouette in her minds eye. What kind of beast stood taller than a man and had antlers as wide as he was tall?

"When the beast tried to leave the mountain, he would instantly find himself at its peak once more. He tried everything to return home, but the mountain held him prisoner."

"That's terrible," Indira whispered.

"Eventually the man accepted his fate and made his home upon the mountaintop. A palace was provided for him. Everything he needed to sustain his life was made available to him. But he was cursed to be a captive in his own home."

Indira's heart ached for that kind of curse. She loved being part of a large family. And although the noise did get to her at times, she didn't think she would like to live alone. Especially not for years!

"As the years passed, his temperament changed into something as bitter as the cold that surrounded him.

"When another entered the sphere of his icy influence, he captured them and sent them to the dungeon of his palace in the snow, never to be released. Word spread to stay away from the mountain, for the Mountain Guardian would capture any who strayed too close."

"Why would he capture people and keep them prisoner?" Indira whispered, afraid to break the spell that Mena's words had created.

"He resented the mortals who lived out their lives below. He could no longer remember his old life after the years on the mountain, but he knew he had been like them at one time."

Indira held her breath. She pondered the words. "Why are you telling me this legend?"

Mena studied Indira's face and eyes. As if she hadn't yet decided whether to tell Indira the rest.

She must have seen something in Indira that she trusted. "It is said that the Mountain Guardian has power over the skies. He can bring rain, or even snow, in places it should not be." She let her words hang between them for several beats.

Indira spoke in a hopeful whisper. "So, if we can find the Mountain Guardian… we might be able to bring the rains back?"

Mena pinched her lips. "There is more, little Indi. The Mountain Guardian is dangerous. He views himself superior to mere mortals. He has a violent temperament that demands respect."

Indira's mind raced to match her increased heart rate. "But he can control the weather? If someone could convince him to help, he could save us all…"

Mena reached for Indira's hand. "Yes, child. But

this is a beast with no love in his heart, even for someone as sweet as you."

"But you showed this to me after hearing about my dream. You believe I… saw this beast? It has to mean something." Her breath quickened. She couldn't keep her eyes off the silhouette in the book that Mena held. It was a rough sketch, but it had antlers. Like the figure in the dream.

"Dreams can mean more than we think." Mena's tone was cautionary now. "This is a gift. But it can also be a curse. The Mountain Guardian is dangerous. He is unlikely to help…"

"But what do I have to lose? I don't want our people to suffer anymore. If I can do something to change… all of this…" Indira gestured toward the door. She could see in her mind's eye the people trudging through another day, wondering whether the rains would ever come again. "…I must try."

To herself she thought, *"And it means I won't have to marry Kian. Probably."*

Mena stood abruptly, more nimbly than Indira thought possible. She rested the book on a nearby table and shuffled out of the room. When she returned, she carried something shiny in the palm of her hand.

"Take this. It will protect you." She rested her hand over Indira's.

Indira felt something pass from Mena's hand to her own. She lowered her gaze to her open palm. A pendant on a thin metal chain glinted in the light. In the center of the flat oval disc was an embossed image of a single rose.

"It's beautiful," she breathed. "But I don't understand…" She met Mena's eyes.

Mena shook her head. "It has been in my possession for many years, but I believe it should belong to you now. It has offered me protection when I have been in danger. It will do the same for you."

Indira opened her mouth to ask how, but Mena interrupted her. "Do not ask questions, child. Appearances can be deceiving. And there are some things we are not meant to understand."

The way Mena said "we" felt more like "you" to Indira, but she didn't argue.

"If you are to embark on this quest, you must prepare and depart at once. We have no time to waste." Urgency lit up Mena's eyes.

Indira's stomach flipped. Was she really going to do this? Was it a terrible idea?

But wasn't marrying Kian a terrible idea?

What if this worked? It would save them all from a depressing future.

Mena supplied Indira with a heavy cloak, heavier than the one she had worn to the Mistress's house that morning, and a pair of sturdy boots. She told Indira to take her mule to carry her to the mountains.

"You may discover help along the way. You may be

on your own the entire time. Once you arrive at the base of the mountains, climb. Do not look back."

"Thank you." Indira threw her arms around Mena's shoulders and squeezed.

She hurried home to gather the other necessary belongings she would need for a long journey. She didn't even know where she was going. Mena told her to head north. That she would find it if she was true of heart.

It all sounded so far-fetched. But if Indira stayed here, she would have to marry Kian. Maybe she was running away from the unwanted union. But she did believe in her heart that she might find deliverance for her home. Her people. Their way of life. She had to try.

"What do you mean you are going on a journey? Where could you possibly need to go?" Indira's mother asked with her hands on her hips and a scowl on her face.

Indira didn't know if she should tell them everything. Would they think she was being irresponsible by leaving? Would they think she was a fool?

"Mistress Mena has asked me to do this for her." It wasn't exactly a lie. Just maybe not the whole truth.

"At least take someone with you. You should not be traveling alone." Her mother nibbled on her thumbnail.

Mistress Mena had been clear that it would be hard enough to convince the Mountain Guardian to help if she went alone. It would be impossible if she brought someone with her. He would feel threatened. They would likely be kept prisoner for the remainder of their days.

Indira filled her cross-body satchel with the cloak, a water pouch, a sparse amount of food wrapped in cloth, and her favorite book. She supposed it was foolish to bring a book, but it helped calm her anxiety when things weren't going well. And she had a feeling she would need it on this journey.

She hugged her parents and waved goodbye to her siblings. She asked her mother and father to not make a big deal about this trip. She would be back in no time. And hopefully when she returned, she would return with rain for their parched lands.

Indira made her way back down the hill toward Mistress Mena's home. She would retrieve her mule and leave at once.

She fiddled with the rose necklace that hung around her neck and tried to push all her worries from her mind. Mistress Mena would not ask her to do something that was impossible. She wouldn't put Indira in harms way if she didn't think the outcome couldn't be positive.

"If only she could come with me. I could use her wisdom and strength," Indira murmured to herself.

Indira heard Kian's voice around the corner. She

groaned. She didn't want to deal with him now. He would ask her about the proposal. She didn't know what she would tell him.

She ducked low and tried to hide behind her hair as she scurried past.

But, of course, he spotted her.

"Excuse me ladies," he said in a formal voice to the handful of giggling girls that gazed at him with love-sick eyes.

He tipped his head and then jogged to catch up to Indira.

She quickened her steps.

He hooked his hand around her arm and tugged it. "Where are you going in such a hurry?" He skimmed her from head to toe with his gaze.

She sighed. "I'm going… to visit Mistress Mena." Her shoulders slumped. She should have thought of some fib to get him to leave her alone. But she was never one to lie so easily.

"I'll walk you there." He straightened his posture and puffed out his chest. He slid his hand down her arm, grasped her hand, then tucked hers into the crook of his own arm.

She knew she should feel all tingly at his touch. Her heart should race. She should blush and giggle, like the other girls. But she saw right through his shallow good looks.

"I must ask you again, my love," he murmured in a low, husky voice. "Will you consent to a union with me?"

She inwardly rolled her eyes. *My love? What did he know about love?*

Her throat squeezed as she tried to think of something to say to put him off without rejecting him outright. If this journey to the Mountain Guardian did not bring the relief her people needed, and if she managed to return at all, she would need to marry him. She had to convince him that she wanted it, at least a little, or else her absence would only send him into the arms of another.

"Kian… I." She batted her eyelashes at him. And instantly hated herself for it. She couldn't string him along. She would reject him. She would make the Mountain Guardian help her. It was the only way.

She pulled her hand from Kian's solid arm. "I can't. My answer is no. Find someone else."

He stopped. His feet froze to the ground. His jaw slightly dropped and there was a look of pure shock in his eyes.

He'd probably never been told no before in his life.

"I'm sorry." She hurried to add. "I must be on my way."

She turned away from him and ran straight for Mistress Mena's house. She didn't even knock. She threw the door open, slammed it shut behind her, and leaned against the door. Her breaths came heavy and fast. She closed her eyes and willed her racing heart and mind to slow.

"You finally told him no, did you?" Mena said from her kitchen.

Indira's eyes flew open. She made her way toward the sound of Mena's voice.

"Yes… how did you know?" she asked the old woman.

Mena tapped the side of her head. "I know many things."

Indira dropped her shoulders and hung her head. Guilt washed over her. Not just because of Kian's reaction, but because of the finality of what it meant for her family. And for herself. Now she must not fail on this quest.

Mena shuffled to stand in front of her. She placed a hand on each of Indira's upper arms. "Do not worry, child. All will be well. You will see. Now, do not waste any more time. Take the mule. Be on your way."

She turned and retrieved a bundle from the table in the corner of her kitchen. Then she handed it to Indira. "For your journey."

Indira opened the cloth package. Inside were four fluffy, fruity muffins. Indira took a sharp breath. "How did you make these?"

"I've been saving an egg and a cup of milk for a special occasion. Take them." She wrapped the package and rested her hands on top of Indira's. "Go."

Indira wrapped the woman in a warm embrace. "Thank you," she whispered.

Mena patted her gently on the back. "See you

soon."

Five

The mule trotted at a surprisingly fast pace across the dry grass lands. As if it knew where to go, it carried Indira due north.

With nothing else to keep her occupied, her mind couldn't help but wander through all the possible scenarios of what might take place. She didn't have a clear vision of what the Guardian looked like, but she had some clues.

She imagined arriving. She would knock on the great icy doors of the Mountain Guardian's castle. The doors would swing open.

She would enter, look all around, and find no one. After some exploring, she would discover him. He would be angry. Drag her to the dungeon. Lock her up forever.

A chill ran down her spine.

No. That was not how it would be. She would be able to appeal some sense of the human that he had once been. Perhaps a code of honor. Or simple pride if he was vain like Kian. He would listen to her petition for assistance. He would acknowledge his ability to assist. He would agree to help her people. Then he would send the rain and she would return in no time to a refreshed land and grateful people.

If only she could arrive faster. The sooner she got this over with, the sooner her people could return to a normal life again.

Even though the mule was faster than Indira had expected, it wasn't as fast as a horse would have been. And even though she wished she could ride a horse for this journey, there were no horses to be found in their village. Not anymore. An hour at the mule's quick pace only took them beyond the grasslands and into the foothills. It would have to do.

Indira had traveled down and upriver in her father's boats many times. She had seen sandy deserts, lush valleys, and beaches that stretched along the sea. She had met many different kinds of people and creatures from many different lands: centaurs, dwarves, naiads, Forest People. But she had never ventured north. Never traveled to the foothills. It was an entirely new experience. She pushed aside the sense of dread that wanted to prevail and forced herself to enjoy the journey and not worry about the destination. Or what she might find upon arrival.

Forests of pine trees filled her nose with a sharp scent. Pinecones cracked beneath the mule's hooves. Fairyberry bushes laden with blue, purple, and red berries hugged the rough trunks of the tall, narrow trees. Wildflowers of every color bloomed in patches where the sun shone through to the forest floor. She even spotted the occasional honey pixie flit from blossom to blossom. Moss covered stones. Fallen logs lined with stair-step mushrooms gave the forest an inviting feel, making her want to rest against the softness for an afternoon nap.

But Indira did not have time for a nap. She urged the mule forward.

Another two hours on the mule's back brought evening. Dusk dimmed the sky eastward. Her stomach grumbled.

She finally slid off the mule's back near a creek. She knew to be watchful for carnivorous plants near the water, though with the small size of the creek she doubted she would come across anything too dangerous.

The mule could graze, and drink. Her own body could rest for a bit. The muscles across her back were tight. Her hands cramped from holding the reins for so long. Her legs felt wobbly beneath her even though she hadn't been using them at all.

She sank to the ground. She opened her pack and pulled out one of Mena's muffins. It smelled delightful. She sank her teeth in, and the sweetness of the fruit and richness of the sponge melted on her tongue. She groaned and closed her eyes. Chewed slowly to savor every bite. Licked her fingers when she was finished. And picked the crumbs off her skirt.

"Well done, Mistress Mena," she said out loud.

The mule lifted his head and stared at her with one eye. He blinked twice, then returned to grazing.

Indira didn't know why she found that so funny. She burst out into laughter. It was like the mule understood her! She laughed for several long minutes. Then the laughter slowly melted into tears.

She was alone in a strange place. She didn't know where she was going. She didn't know if or when she would ever return. She didn't know if her family, her people, would survive any more trials like the thunderbird encounter.

She sucked in a deep breath, held it for a moment, then released it all at once.

"Pull yourself together, Indi. You will do this." She pulled herself from the ground.

"Alright, friend," she spoke to the mule, "let's keep going."

Riding the mule again was worse than walking might have been. Her muscles protested the stiff position and lack of movement. But it would be faster for this animal to jog through the woods than for herself to wander on her own two feet.

Night fell. The steepness of the hills intensified. The

shadows beneath the trees deepened. The mule's gait slowed to a steady walk up the steepening hillside.

Indira nodded off, something she never would have imagined to be possible. She caught her head bobbing several times and scolded herself for not paying closer attention to her surroundings. She wasn't an adventurer. She didn't know much about the plants or animals that surrounded her. For all she knew she could have a pack of wolves stalking her right now and not even know it.

As if it had read her thoughts, a wolf let out a long, high howl into the air. A chorus of howls returned the call.

"Great. Time to go faster." She kicked at the mule's sides.

The mule protested with a huff out of his nose. Another gentle kick gave him the encouragement he needed, and he increased his speed a little.

Indira tried to listen for any sounds of the wolves. The mule didn't seem spooked or upset. Hopefully the wolves that had been talking to one another in their own language were far away from them.

As the mule carried her from the foothills to the mountain itself, they gained elevation. The air became crisp. Indira awkwardly pulled her cloak from her pack with one hand while holding on to the reins with the other. She did her best to wrap the cloak over her shoulders and clasp it closed with her one free hand.

Patches of frozen white snow appeared here and

there where the sun never reached them during the day. Indira could see her breath in front of her face, as well as the mule's.

The mule slowed again. She didn't prod him faster.

According to Mistress Mena, once she approached the mountain, the Guardian should appear, or she should be transported to his ice palace in the blink of an eye, or something.

Should she call out for him? Should she stay quiet? She wasn't exactly sure what she should do.

The clasp of the cloak came loose. It slipped off her shoulders and floated to the forest floor behind her.

"Oh!" she cried. "Stop, mule." She commanded the creature.

She slid from his back. Her legs buckled beneath her. She hadn't realized her feet had become numb both from lack of use and from the frigid temperatures.

Her hands scraped against a thorny vine that grew on the forest floor. She cried out as a crimson line appeared on her palm.

The sound startled the mule. His ears pricked and he snorted out his nose. He stamped his hooves against the ground.

"It's fine." She tried to gain her feet. She rested a hand on the mule's side to steady herself.

The mule's skin flinched beneath her touch. All four of his feet left the ground in quick succession with his jump. He let out an alarming bray. Then he took off at full speed down the mountain. Away from Indira.

"Wait! Come back!" Indira cried. She was back on the ground, standing on her knees. "Don't leave me here all alone!" she hollered.

It was no use. The animal was gone.

Indira crawled to retrieve her cloak and threw it over her shoulders once more. This time she used two hands to clip it tight around her neck and made sure it was secure. Then she fell to a sitting position and sighed.

"Now what?"

A branch somewhere beyond her line of vision cracked. She jumped. An owl hooted in the opposite direction. Crickets chirped and frogs croaked. Insects buzzed around.

She had always thought that a forest at night would be quiet and eerie. But there were plenty of insects and other creatures that lived in the cold on this mountain. She wished she could see them all. Catalogue them to tell her siblings about. But she couldn't see any of them. Only hear them. And they were loud. So loud that she definitely wouldn't be able to hear an animal, like a wolf, sneak up on her and drag her off for a midnight snack.

She shivered. Not just from the cold, this time. She studied her surroundings. She wasn't about to trapse through the woods all alone in the middle of the night with nothing but a satchel that only carried a book, some muffins, and a few extra sets of undergarments.

Why hadn't she brought a weapon of some kind?

The thought made her laugh. "A weapon? What, Indi, you're going to fight off a pack of ravenous wolves all by yourself?" She snapped her mouth closed. She did not need to be talking to herself now! What if that made the wolves track her even better?

There had to be someplace to safe and out of the weather to shelter for the night. She would continue to climb the mountain in the light of day. She managed to gain her feet and turned in a slow circle.

One of the large trees nearby had a hollow spot at its base. It looked kind of like the triangle tents some of the vendors used at market. It would have to do.

She hobbled her way over on tingly feet and crawled into the entrance. She wrapped her cloak tightly around her entire body and leaned against the inside of the tree with her knees pulled to her chest and her arms wrapped tightly around her legs. Her pack sat atop her feet in an attempt to protect them from the cold, at least a little.

"I just have to survive until morning," she told herself.

Six

reams of roaring wild beasts, snarling wolves, and ice encrusted roses plagued Indira until the cold temperature made her shiver so much that she couldn't stay asleep any longer.

She allowed her eyes to stay open and scan the surroundings outside her hideout.

Deep snow blanketed the forest. Fuzzy ice coated every surface. Indira was only spared because of the protection of the tree she had slept in. She pulled her cloak tighter around her body and shivered. Her teeth chattered. Her breath fogged the air in front of her face.

"No time to waste, I suppose," she murmured to herself. A deep, fortifying breath stung her lungs instead of giving her the mental boost she needed. "Note to self, don't breathe deep in the cold."

She kicked the ankle-height snow out of the opening of the tree hideout. Her muscles protested as she stretched into a standing position with one hand against the frozen tree trunk for support. Between the ride on the mule all day yesterday and sleeping curled up in a tiny ball most of the night, she was surprised her body even obeyed her wishes at all.

"It's a good thing Mistress Mena supplied me with these heavy boots," she said to herself through her chattering teeth. "I should have brought some mittens, though, too." She stuffed her hands underneath her arms inside the cloak and faced the steep slope of the mountain.

"Now I just need to find the Guardian's palace and get this over with before I freeze to death!"

Indira resisted another deep breath. She didn't realize how much she sighed until it became painful!

"Let's get this over with." She trudged through the deep snow through the trees. It gave her the boost of energy she needed to keep going.

The snow muffled the normal daytime sounds of the forest. Besides the crunch of her boots in the snow, and her own heavy, painful breathing, the forest was eerily quiet. The way she had expected it to sound during the night.

"At least I won't walk in circles since it's obvious where I've already been."

As if the mountain heard her comment, great fluffy snowflakes fell from between the treetops. Indira stopped and turned her face toward them. They tickled her cheeks when they landed. One stuck to her eyelashes. She turned in a circle with a big smile on her face.

"It's so beautiful!" she hollered with a laugh.

The snow thickened. Blistering cold wind picked up and made the snowflakes dance. It blew the snow already on the ground in swirls.

Indira's smile faded after she watched the magic of it for a few minutes. Her tracks had been covered. She no longer knew where she had already been.

Was this the work of the Mountain Guardian? Was he trying to keep her off his mountain? At least that meant she was in the right place!

"You can't stop me that easily!" she yelled into the sky. "I'm still coming!"

She stood tall and marched with determined steps through the snow and up the mountainside.

The wind blew in her face.

She hunched over and protected her face with her arm against the blowing snow.

The snowfall became heavier. Everything around her was shrouded in a curtain of white.

She clenched her jaw and persevered. She would not let this stop her. She would do whatever it took to find the Mountain Guardian and get him to release the water on her people's land once again.

There was no track to follow. No road that led to the top of the mountain. No path or trail marker to tell her she was headed in the right direction. She trusted her gut that she wasn't wandering in a blizzard in circles.

Her feet became numb again. Her fingertips burned from the icy cold. Did she even have a nose anymore? The snow stabbed at her cheeks. Ice built up on her eyelashes, and the hairs inside her nostrils froze with each inhale.

"I. Will. Not. Stop." She huffed out between breaths as she took ever-slower steps through the ever-deepening snow up the ever-steepening mountain.

Suddenly the blizzard stopped. The sky became blue again.

Indira froze. She lifted her eyes skyward. Maybe the Guardian had heard her words?

She welcomed the hopefully-not-momentary pause in the storm and rushed onward. She had climbed a great distance in the few hours she had been hiking. The ice palace had to be around here somewhere.

Well, it could be on totally the other side of the mountain, but Mistress Mena had said to travel north and climb the mountain and she would find it. She had taken the instructions literally.

Warm air greeted Indira a little while later. She was

pretty sure she no longer had fingers or toes anymore, by that point.

The absence of bitter cold on her face made her cheeks hurt more. Up ahead she could spot green through all the white snow-covered landscape.

"A garden?" she wondered out loud.

It gave her renewed energy that she might be able to find relief from the cold before night fell again. She hurried ahead to investigate.

She had expected the Mountain Guardian to live in a palace made of ice, since he brought cold wherever he went. So, she was absolutely stunned when the snow came to an abrupt end around a lush green garden. A garden that surrounded a very not-icy palace.

The castle was made from smooth-cut stone blocks. It had arched windows, slate shingled roofs, and even a couple of circular turrets with pointed tops. The castle stretched four stories high. The doors that she could see were oversized. The stained-glass windows gave color to the otherwise gray exterior. Vines with delicate pink flowers grew up one side of the palace and all the way to the top of one of the turrets.

Indira stood with her eyes wide and stared. Then she remembered how cold she was. There would be time to explore the gardens later, she was sure. For now, she needed to find a fire. And a warm blanket. And something hot to drink. Before her body shut down from the exposure to the cold that she had endured.

She took stumbling steps down the cobblestone path that led to the front doors of the palace. Tall leafy trees lined either side of the road. She spotted large orange balls hanging from the branches. Citrus fruit? Her mouth watered. How long had it been since she'd eaten fresh fruit of any kind?

Behind the tree-lined walkway the garden stretched all the way to the edge of the castle and around its sides. Did it circumvent the castle entirely?

Between the tree trunks and low hanging branches Indira spied statues sprinkled throughout the gardens. They appeared to be statues of people frozen in place.

Ha! Frozen- like ice! She laughed to herself. Then her stomach sank like it had a rock in it. What if they really were frozen people? Maybe he didn't throw people in a dungeon…

She forced her mind to focus on her surroundings instead of inventing worst-cast-scenarios about her soon to be encounter with the fearsome Mountain Guardian.

Moss grew in between the cobblestones of the road, giving the whole place a welcoming, romantic feel. A well-placed bench along the path would make for a perfect place to relax.

She pressed forward.

Branches formed a sort of tunnel overhead. It cast everything around her in shadow, but not so dark as to be ominous or frightening.

Her foot stumbled against one of the cobblestones. She caught herself before she fell flat on her face, thank goodness. Her eyes darted toward the castle. Hopefully the Guardian hadn't seen that. It wasn't very confidence inspiring to see someone trip over their own feet, was it? She needed to appear poised and sure of herself if she was to convince the Guardian to listen to her words and not throw her immediately into his dungeon.

Her eyes wandered to the towers. Or lock her in one of the towers for the rest of her days.

Or become one of the frozen statues in the garden. She shivered at the thought.

Though it was like climbing another mountain, she managed to arrive at the top of dozens of steps that led to the grand entrance of the castle without tripping again. She would take that as a win.

Huge mahogany doors marked the entrance to the castle. Brass fixtures and flowery designs trimmed the edges. She took a deep breath.

It didn't hurt to breathe anymore! Another win.

She scolded herself for the random thought and focused on the task at hand. She raised her hand toward the brass knocker and gripped it tight. She pulled it outward and paused before banging it against the door.

Would he be there? Would he help her? There was only one way to find out.

Seven

The palace may not have been formed from ice, but the atmosphere was just as cold.

No one came to the door when she used the brass knocker to announce her presence.

No one greeted her when she pushed the huge door open enough to slip through into the grand entryway.

The furniture in the rooms she could see had all been covered with white cloths.

Dust coated the rich mahogany staircase that curved and widened as it descended from the second floor.

Cobwebs decorated the corners of the smooth rainbow agate balustrades topped with a wide mahogany railing. More spiderwebs hung from the long unlit chandelier that hung slightly askew above her head.

It wasn't only the floor that had been tiled in pristine marble. The walls had marble tiles all the way to the second story ceiling. A pattern of greens, blues, and creams accented with more brass fixtures.

She tiptoed across the sparkling marble tiled floor toward a sitting room off to one side. The room she found was magnificently furnished with armchairs, sofas, footstools, end tables, and sideboards all arranged in front of a fireplace taller than Indira. She stood in the doorway for a moment to take it all in. Protective cloths did not cover the items in this space. It appeared to have been recently dusted, as well. And the knickknacks on the fireplace mantle had been arranged just so.

"So, somebody *does* live here," she murmured. She took a tentative step into the room.

When her foot crossed the threshold, the fireplace burst to life with a blazing fire.

Indira jumped and screeched. How had that happened? Was it some kind of dark magic or something?

But another part of her mind remembered that she was quite cold. She rushed forward and kneeled in front of the fire close enough to feel the heat without burning herself.

She held her hands toward the flames. She relished the heat on her face and arms. She stayed there for so long that her face felt hot by the time she was satisfied and moved away from the blazing fire.

The new warmth of her skin and clothes and the exertions of the past twenty-four hours left Indira feeling completely drained. The sofa in front of the fireplace had several plush pillows resting on it. A soft angora wool blanket had been draped carefully over one end.

"Don't mind if I do," she whispered as she yawned and collapsed on the couch. She covered herself with the warm blanket and curled on her side, her face toward the cozy fire.

Her eyes sunk closed at the same time as she heard a shuffle through the door of the room. But she couldn't pry her eyes open again to discover the source.

When Indira awoke, the sky outside the windows was dark. It was nighttime, but what hour she did not know. She sat up and stretched. She sighed. She was comfortably warm and felt safe from the dangers of the wilderness that surrounded the castle.

Her stomach rumbled. She looked down at it as if she could discover what it desired. She already knew, of course. She removed her pack from across her body and opened it to eat another of Mena's muffins.

"What? Where'd they go?" She peered into her bag. She had brough practically nothing with her. Her book was still there. But the food she had carried along with her was missing.

Her eyes darted around the room. Had someone taken it from her? Or perhaps it had fallen out when she stumbled through the snowy woods.

Her shoulders slumped. "Now what am I going to do?" Then she scolded herself. "If someone lives here, that means there's a kitchen. I just need to find it and then I'll have something to eat."

She stood to leave the room and search the palace for a kitchen or pantry of some kind. She would even return to the garden and pick some oranges off the trees if she must.

But it turned out to not be necessary. For there behind the couch, on the sideboard against the back wall of the room, lay an elaborate arrangement of food and drink. Like someone had prepared a meal for an honored guest.

Had that been there when she fell asleep earlier in the afternoon? She didn't think so, but maybe she had been too distracted by her immediate need for warmth to have noticed.

She hurried toward the table. Steam rose from a white, plump teapot with a golden handle and purple lid. She rested her hand around it. It was hot. This had been put here recently.

"Then I guess it's for me?" she whispered. She paused. Held her breath. If the Guardian knew she was here, and he put this food out for her, then there was no harm in eating it. Right?

But what if he didn't know she was here. What if a servant put this here for him to eat when he returned from… wherever Mountain Guardian's go when they're away from home? She could be accused of stealing…

Her stomach made another loud, hungry noise.

She shrugged. "There's enough to share!"

She poured herself a serving of rosemary tea in a matching white teacup with a gold handle and purple skirt.

A stack of two small, matching plates rested at one end of the buffet. She carefully took one and perused her food options. Fresh strawberries, a bowl of cherries, miniature carrots with their tops still on, grape-sized tomatoes, cubes of cheese, cured meats, crackers, miniature cakes, wildflower honey to drizzle on flatbread. The choices were too much!

"I'll just take one of everything!" she said with a small smile. "Except maybe this. I'll have two of you, please," she said to the pile of chocolate truffles at the end of the sideboard table.

She placed her plate and cup on a small tray and lifted it off the table. "Now, where should I sit to eat?"

It didn't seem right to sit on the sofa, but there wasn't another more practical option. She settled herself on the sofa with the tray in her lap and dug into the food in front of her.

When she had eaten half of it, she stopped suddenly. Guilt washed over her. The people in her village were practically starving and here she was gorging on delicacies that they hadn't seen in a very long time.

She stopped and returned the half-eaten glazed scone onto her plate. No. She would only eat enough to sustain her. Nothing more. In fact…

She looked over her shoulders. She peeked out the door into the lobby. No one was around. She hurried back to the display of luxurious food. She removed her book from her bag and set it on the table. She emptied bowl after plate after tray of everything into her bag until it was filled to the brim.

"If he won't help me, then at least I'll be able to bring some food back for my family," she said to herself. "And maybe some fruit from the garden, too," she pondered.

From somewhere far on the other side of the palace came a frightful noise caused by something enormous.

Indira froze. Was it the Mountain Guardian? Did he know what she was doing?

The clock in the entry hall struck the hour. She felt like it called her name, accusing her of her crime.

"Innnnn-deeeeee! Innnnnn-deeeeee!" it repeated twelve times.

Midnight. She shivered. Something about the hour

made her uneasy.

She was half tempted to slip out the door and hurry back the way she had come. But one meal's worth of food would not solve the larger problem her people faced. She must speak with the Guardian. She must make him see their plight. Take action. Save them.

She marched into the entry of the palace. She stood right in the middle. She turned in a full circle, placed her hands around her mouth, and yelled.

"Hello? I need to speak with you at once. It is a matter of life and death!"

She paused. Waited. Listened. No sounds made their way to her ears.

"He has to be here. Somewhere. And if he won't come to me, then I will just go find him."

She marched toward the wide curved staircase that led to the second floor.

"Ready or not, here I come," she murmured underneath her breath.

Eight

Moonlight shone through the windows from outside, though it did little to illuminate the inside of the palace. And Indira soon discovered that wandering in a dark castle, alone, in the middle of the night, with some mythical being said to have a violent temper lurking in the shadows somewhere, was not something that she wished to do.

She returned to the couch in front of the fire and chose to wait until daylight to find the Guardian. A couple more bites of cheese and fruit satisfied her hunger enough for her to return to the sofa to sleep until daytime.

No dreams interrupted the few hours she slept. The same supply of food greeted her in the morning.

With no change of clothes, no obvious place to wash, and no mirror, her usual routine of the morning had to be set aside. There was nothing to do except explore.

Indira wandered around the castle for the better part of the morning. The Guardian had to be in here somewhere. If he was even real.

"If Mistress Mena believes, then so do I." She squared her shoulders and pondered where to search first.

The Guardian would not be found wandering around the first floor, which was typically reserved for entertaining guests. At least, that's what she believed about castles. She had never been in one before, so she couldn't be sure, but the logic was sound. But she had neither seen nor heard any signs of him in her quick perusal of the ground floor.

"Second floor it is," Indira murmured to herself.

The wide staircase curved in a grand arch and her hand slid effortlessly along the wood railing, which left a layer of dust on her fingertips.

Once at the top of the stairs Indira sighed and began her search. How hard could a beast be to find, anyway?

The walls inside the first room that she came across had been hung with mirrors of every shape and size. She would have liked to see her own reflection in one, because she knew she probably looked frightful, but every single mirror had been broken. All of them were cracked, smashed, and some had no more glass in them whatsoever. The pieces lay in heaps along the entire perimeter of the room. No furniture adorned this space. There were dozens and dozens of broken mirrors in an empty room.

She didn't linger. The Guardian was not to be found there.

The next room in that wing of the castle was a picture gallery. Single sitting chairs had been carefully placed around the space to allow leisurely, solitary viewings of the paintings. It was obvious the Guardian wasn't there, either, but Indira was entranced by the pieces of art.

She had seen many stunning art pieces on her trips with her father, but their own village did not produce much in the way of paintings. Her home only had a couple in her father's office.

Here was an entire gallery for her viewing pleasure. She wandered around the room and gazed at the magnificent paintings. Landscapes, fantastical creatures, magical sunsets, brilliant night skies. Did the Guardian paint these? Or did he acquire them somehow? Maybe one of his prisoners was an artist.

Wait. She didn't know for sure he held prisoners. Those were the tales, but not all tales were true. She shouldn't jump to any conclusions unless she found out for herself. Still. Where had these stunning pieces come from?

Realizing she was wasting her time staring at art

instead of trying to plead with the Guardian to save her people, she hurried to the next room.

She found herself in the doorway of another sitting room, like the ones she had seen on the first floor, with covered furniture and a layer of dust over every surface. This room had been long unlived in. The next three rooms were much the same.

A back set of stairs, likely used by servants to stay out of sight of the castle residents, carried her to the third floor. Did the castle have servants? The legend said the Mountain Guardian was cursed to live alone. Did that mean no one else lived here at all? The dust that coated everything certainly attested to the fact that most of the palace had stood abandoned for a very long time. What if it really was a myth? What if there was no Guardian?

"Then you'll go home. Figure something else out…"

Like marry Kian. She shuddered.

She visited a room filled with a variety of instruments of every kind. Enough for a full orchestra, but melancholy underneath thick layers of dust.

Another picture gallery took up the room beside the music room. As much as she wished to gaze at more magnificent works of art, she could peruse them some other time. Unless she left before she had the chance. Maybe she'd find her way back to this castle again someday?

She passed several large guest suites. Again, with the

furniture covered. No one had entered any of these rooms in ages.

No signs of the Mountain Guardian, either.

Perhaps the Mountain Guardian would be found on the fourth floor. She looked at the ceiling as if she could see through the floor to discover his whereabouts. She sighed.

Another wide staircase at one end of the palace carried her to the fourth floor. Would she find him up here? If he was real, he would be up here.

She turned right at the top of the stairs. This appeared to be a residential wing. And it appeared to be made for a woman. Everything was decorated with the finest fabrics, exotic flowers, and fanciest laces she had ever seen. The furniture was dainty and feminine. The doorways were even a bit shorter than most of the other ones. Like they had been built for a more petite person. Much like herself.

A bouquet of fresh colorful roses stood on a table beside the main entrance to the woman's suite. Indira paused to bury her nose into them. They smelled heavenly.

But the space was too small for the Guardian. Too cramped. If he truly did have antlers, the Guardian would certainly not fit through the doors.

The final wing of the castle had been decorated in a much more masculine manner. Darker wood, rougher fabrics, drawn curtains. And the floors were well worn as if they had been paced back and forth upon for decades.

Indira's heart raced. She was about to find the Guardian, she was sure.

She hesitated when she reached the door to a room that she was certain would be his living quarters. The other parts of this wing had mirrored the feminine side. And this is where the living quarters would be.

She knocked with three sharp taps.

She held her breath.

A shuffling noise came from the other side of the door.

Nothing happened.

She frowned. What was he waiting for?

She knocked again, firmer this time.

A thump came from the other side.

"I can hear you, you know. You might as well open the door!" she hollered through the keyhole. If only she could see through the gap between the door and the frame. But it was too narrow.

A rough, low, menacing voice spoke on the other side. "Go away."

She jumped, placed a hand on her chest to slow her now racing heart and steadied her breathing.

"I need your help. My people need your help. May I please have an audience with you?" She stood tall and spoke formally.

She waited.

"Well?" She urged him to respond.

"No." His voice was firm. His answer final.

She knew she shouldn't argue, but she refused to take no for an answer.

"I know you can help. Our land is dry. Our people are thirsty. Hungry. Our river is dried up. I was told you could send the rain back to our lands. Save our people. Please, you have to try!"

A grunt came from inside the room. Further away from the door this time. Would he respond?

"I won't help. I told you to leave. I will make you if I must. Now go." He barked through the door at her.

"That's it? You're just going to let us all die? What kind of a guardian are you?" she scoffed at his brusque reply.

He huffed a breath out of his nose. It reminded her of the mule she rode here. Maybe he was as stubborn as a mule, but he was in for a rude awakening. For she was stubborn as one, too.

"I'm not leaving until you agree to help." She folded her arms and planted her feet on the plush carpeted floor.

He growled.

She waited. Again.

"I prefer to be left alone," he grumbled.

"I prefer to not starve to death," she countered.

Suddenly the door swung open in front of her. She jumped and scooted backwards until she was pressed against the opposite wall.

Her wide eyes took in his strange appearance. They rose from his moose-like cloven hooves and up his wide fur covered legs. The dark brown fur transitioned into matching dark brown feathers where his hips met his waist. His torso, though human in shape, was covered in feathers and wider than any human man would have. His broad chest led to even broader shoulders and a thick neck hidden beneath more layers of feathers. His feathered arms hung nearly to his knees. Instead of wings, they ended in human shaped, feather covered hands.

Her eyes rose higher up his neck to his head where his body appeared to be half-moose, half-eagle, but man shaped. His head was a strange combination of eagle and moose. There was nothing human about it at all.

Fur surrounded his moose-like eyes. They blended into feathers on the remainder of his head. His nose extended forward like a moose's nose but ended in the sharp black beak of an eagle. And like the silhouette in her dream, and the sketch in the book, a set of moose antlers bigger than Indira had ever imagined rested on top of his head.

When she had finished scanning him, her eyes met the eyes of the Guardian.

She gulped.

As he growled at her, ice crystals fogged his breath and dropped to the floor like shards of glass. Frost climbed the door frame where he rested one of his hands.

His dark eyes bore down on her. He lifted his nose

in the air as if he couldn't stand the smell of her.

"I said. Go. Away." He spoke so deeply that she could feel the rumblings from her head to her toes.

She stood frozen against the wall. She wiggled her fingers and toes. Maybe not frozen, literally, although she didn't doubt he could do that to her if he wanted. But frozen from fear. Or apprehension. She didn't think he would harm her. His eyes seemed too kind for that.

He squinted his animal-like eyes and glared at her. Through clenched teeth from his oddly shaped face he said, "If you don't go of your own accord, I will make you. Do not test me on this."

Indira was never one to stand down in the face of a challenge. And that sure sounded like a challenge to her!

"Is that so?" she said with force. "Help me, and I'll leave. That would be easier than whatever else you have in mind, wouldn't it?" She stared right back at him.

He stepped closer. She sucked in a sharp breath and pressed harder into the wall.

"I will not help anyone. Please leave." His unblinking eyes were as cold as ice.

Indira looked away. Was she being foolish? Would he harm her if she pressed him too much? Was he violent like Mistress Mena had warned?

The fight left her. She slouched.

"Fine," she whispered. Her eyes filled with tears,

and she turned to leave. "I'll go. But know that my people will die if you don't help them."

He huffed, reentered his room, and slammed the door shut behind him. The sound and vibration made her jump.

She retraced her steps to the front entrance of the palace and through the front door. Her feet carried her down the front steps. Her breath came fast, and her heart raced. How was she supposed to save her people without the Mountain Guardian's help? Hopelessness weighed down on her back like a heavy load.

Expecting to find herself on the straight, cobblestone path that led toward the gate and the wintry forest beyond, Indira received a surprise to discover a different scene before her.

Had she left through a different door than the one she had entered? This didn't look familiar.

Behind her stood the front of the castle, exactly as she had seen it the day before. The massive door was the same one she had pushed open to enter the palace.

But when she turned around to face the path that should lead her away from the castle, confusion left her palms clammy and her throat tight.

The cobblestone road that she walked on when she arrived had been straight. Now, however, it curved away from the wintry wood outside the garden walls.

Indira took timid steps forward. How had the road... changed? Where was the exit now?

She looked back over her shoulder at the castle.

Why had she let that beast of a Mountain Guardian intimidate her so? She normally stood up for herself. She didn't back down from a challenge. Ever.

It didn't make any sense. She followed the now-curved path into the heart of the garden instead of into the forest and toward her home.

Every variety of flower imaginable blossomed in the garden. Some of them should bloom during different seasons from one another. She inhaled the sweet fragrance from the wide variety.

The path upon which she walked was no longer cobblestone, but low-growing grass. It was soft beneath her feet. The sounds of bird songs and bees buzzing gave her a calm feeling.

Her mind cleared, as if her surroundings lifted a fog she hadn't noticed before.

"I don't want to leave," she murmured to herself. "I will not let the Mountain Guardian boss me around. Just because he is big and mean-looking, and I am only a petite woman doesn't mean he is stronger than me. Maybe physically, yes. But my will cannot be broken that easily."

She stopped in front of a bush laden with dozens of beautiful crimson roses. She touched one of their delicate petals with a finger. It was velvet against her skin. She gently cupped her hand beneath it and leaned close. She breathed in its sweet scent and sighed.

"I will not leave until he helps me," she promised the rose.

And promised herself.

Nine

When she turned away from the rose bush to wander the maze-like garden and contemplate her next steps, a new path had opened for her. Like magic. What was this place?

The new path led straight back to the castle door. Like the castle wanted her to stay.

Whatever this strangeness was, it didn't matter. The only thing that mattered was that she desperately needed the Guardian's help. He could deny her all he wanted. She would fight and fight until he gave in. Only he could provide relief for her people.

Indira returned to the parlor where she had found relief from the elements the previous day.

The Mountain Guardian would have to physically

carry her away if he really wanted her to leave.

She munched on some of the food that she had piled into her bag. She stared into the fire.

How had he made her leave earlier? One minute she was as stubborn as a mule, and the next she was running away in tears.

She paused her chewing. Her back stiffened.

Did he have some way of pushing his will onto another? Was it possible that he had, in fact, *made* her leave?

Boy would he be surprised when he discovered that she was still in his palace. Besides, it *was* as if the castle had wanted her to stay. Not that a castle could want anything. But the path had changed to keep her here. It had returned her to the palace.

She retrieved her book from where she had stuck it in the ties of her dress and relaxed on the sofa in front of the low-burning fire. The room was the perfect temperature. Where the fire had been blazing the day before, it was comfortable now. She didn't need to warm her freezing fingers and toes. She only needed a quiet place to read and sleep. The parlor provided her with those needs.

Her dreams were filled with the smells from the garden. With the images from the picture gallery. And with the shards of glass in the mirror room.

At the center of the mirror room stood a single circular pedestal table.

At the center of the table a strange light illuminated the hourglass. The sand continued to slide from the top to the bottom. It had changed since she had seen it before. Less sand filled the top. More piled in the bottom.

For breakfast, she ate a small portion of the remaining food from her bag. Surely, she would discover a kitchen or pantry that day. But just in case the Guardian did throw her out of the castle, she wanted to have something to eat for her journey home. It would no longer be enough to share with her family.

A shadow filled the doorway to the parlor.

She stood and faced the Mountain Guardian.

"I thought I told you to leave," he growled at her. His voice today was much more menacing.

Pressure gripped her head. Her mind swam with the thought that she should leave. It pushed against her own thoughts. Tried to push its way forward. But she resisted.

"I told you I am staying until you help." She stood tall and firm, though her hands were clasped tight in front of her.

He questioned her in a low, nearly inaudible tone. "Are you inept? Do you not understand the situation?" He lowered his antlered head to enter the room, then stood to his full height once inside.

She didn't budge. She tipped her head back so she could look him in the eye.

He peered down his moose-like nose at her. "You.

Will. Leave."

The force of his words struck her. She gasped.

She gritted her teeth. "No."

He growled.

"My people need help. I'm not leaving." She folded her arms and stuck out her chin. *The stubborn Indira look*, as her family called it.

The Guardian whipped around and left the room so quickly that she startled and took a step back. She bumped into the sideboard and the dishes rattled. She steadied herself with one hand on either side.

His roar echoed through the castle as he bounded up the stairs five or six at a time.

A door slammed high above her head.

"At least he didn't literally throw me out," she sighed to herself. She could imagine him picking her up by the back of her clothes and tossing her out the door like unwanted garbage.

The image struck her as funny for some reason, and she started to giggle. She covered her mouth with her hand, but it was no use. She laughed for real.

"Perhaps the beast has finally met his match!" She smiled. "Now, what am I going to do while I wait for him to change his mind?"

She pondered her options.

She could barge her way up the stairs and into his space and demand that he help her. But harsh words never proved effective when trying to persuade someone to change their mind about something.

The better option would be to win him over with her kindness. Let him see that she wasn't planning to leave until he helped.

Her heart twinged. Her people needed help *now*. But the situation couldn't become much worse than it already was back home. Could it?

If the Guardian couldn't, or wouldn't, help, then they would be no worse off than they had been when she left. The worst that would happen would be that he refused.

Something in the back of her mind whispered that the worst that could happen would be he threw her in a dungeon and never let her go.

It didn't matter. She was determined. She would remain until she convinced him to assist, or she would never return home.

Now she needed to discover the best way to prove that she meant it.

She hadn't had the chance to explore the first floor of the palace yet. Once she had assessed the layout and the options before her, she would make a plan to win the Guardian over to her way of thinking.

She smiled to herself. Maybe she could be *so* kind and thoughtful and sweet that it would annoy him so much that he would agree to help just to get rid of her! It was certainly worth a try.

Just as she expected, the other rooms around the perimeter of the lobby were long unused sitting rooms, parlors, and tea rooms. But a hallway stretched beyond them down the center of the castle toward the back.

The candle tray in her hand cast long shadows down the dark hall. Cobwebs decorated the unlit sconces and corners. Dust coated the wainscotting and the smooth wood floor. All the doors along the hallway were closed. No natural light entered the place whatsoever.

The first door she tried was locked. She moved on. The second one opened into a powder room with a low counter, a wash basin, and an oval mirror hanging on the wall. A small ottoman with tassels on all four corners, and feet that resembled animal paws, rested in front of the counter, ready for a person to sit upon it and gaze at their own reflection in the mirror.

Maybe she should take a peek. She didn't sit on the stool but stood in front of the mirror. She was short enough that she could see from her head to her knees reflected off the smooth surface.

She grimaced. She was a sight! Her hair was tangled and frizzy. A dirt smudge on one cheek resembled a bruise. Her clothes were wrinkled. When she looked down, the hem of her pale skirt had a wide ribbon of mud stains around the entire circumference.

Maybe she did need to get cleaned up! She lowered herself to the ottoman. The items carefully arranged on the table were exactly what she needed. A tall pitcher stood beside the bowl for washing. She poured in fresh water, dipped a washcloth into it, and scrubbed the dirt from her face. Her almond-brown skin looked clean once more. No more imposter bruises.

She used the wide tooth comb to detangle her black hair, then spritzed it with a rose scented spray that helped tame the frizz. Her natural waves returned and draped over her shoulders and down her back.

"What about these clothes, though?"

As she studied her reflection, she saw an armoire tucked into the corner of the room in the shadows, furthest from the door.

She stood and approached the pale wooden furniture. She pulled open one of the mint green doors and discovered a closet full of clothing hanging on a bar fixed across the top.

She sorted through the items. Men's shirts, children's play clothes, a woman's nightgown. Shoes lined the bottom in a variety of shapes, sizes, and styles. She flipped through the clothing again and selected a dress that should fit her if she tied up the skirt a little.

She donned the lightweight nearly white chemise underdress. The cap sleeves covered her shoulders and a tie around the neckline helped her secure it at a modest height on her chest. She covered the underlayer with a dusty pink colored overdress that had laces on the bodice in the front and back. Flexible boning around her ribcage offered support without being stifling. Colorful brocade trim gave the dress a decorative, but not too extravagant, touch. And the skirt opened in the front to reveal the underlayer.

"There." She turned every which way to examine her reflection. The skirt swished in a satisfying way that made Indira grin. The color of the overdress looked perfect against her light brown skin. She smiled at her reflection. "Now I look presentable. Maybe the Guardian will see that I'm not just a lost girl seeking handouts, but a confidant woman with a desire for him to do what is right."

At the end of the hall, Indira found a pair of double doors. She pushed them both open inward. She sucked in a breath. Her hand flew to her mouth. Stretched in front of her was the largest library she had ever seen!

Books lined shelves from floor to ceiling. And the ceilings were tall! Ladders on rails that could slide around the space were placed at regular intervals.

Couches for lounging and reading were arranged just so, with comfy pillows and cozy blankets.

The entire back wall of the library was floor to ceiling windows. It looked out on the vast garden of trees, shrubs, flowers, fruits, and more. Another set of double doors that mirrored the ones she stood beside led from the library into the garden. A basket even sat beside the door, as if inviting the patron to carry a blanket and some books outside for their enjoyment.

"This is… magical!" she whispered. She slid into the room. Her soft steps made no noise on the lush carpet.

She turned to her left and ran a hand along the spines of so many books as she made her way around the curved wall.

"It's like something from a dream!"

When she made her way to the window-wall, she stood and looked out at the garden for several long minutes. Then she returned to explore the vast library.

In one corner stood a round table with a single pedestal leg beneath it. It held several knickknacks. But what caught her off guard was that one of the knickknacks was an hourglass.

She was tempted to turn it upside down. But with the strange way things had been going since she arrived, she wasn't sure that was such a good idea.

What would happen when the sand ran out?

Ten

"Innnn-deee! Innnn-deee!" The grandfather clock struck her name twelve times, for noon instead of midnight this time.

The call broke her out of her stare at the hourglass that perfectly matched the one she had dreamt about twice now. She shook her head to clear her thoughts. It was one little item in a vast palace filled with all kinds of curiosities. It was merely a coincidence that she had dreamt of one before. And besides, how many different styles of hourglasses could there really be? They probably all pretty much looked like that one. Right?

She backed away from the table, exited the library,

and gently closed the doors. Her hand gripped the brass handle for an extra beat.

"I'll be back," she whispered. To the room? The doors? The books?

Her stomach rumbled.

"Time to find the kitchen." She veered down a back hallway that logic told her would lead to a kitchen.

Sure enough, some stone stairs greeted her that led downward instead of up. She descended into a cool stone space that appeared to be a fully functioning palace kitchen big enough to prepare food for dozens and dozens of people.

At the back of the kitchen stood a cellar pantry that descended a little bit further below ground level to keep the food stores cool. Rough wood shelves lined the brick walls from ceiling to floor.

She was surprised to find that it wasn't that well stocked after all. But there were some dried fruits, hard dry crackers tucked inside a metal canister, aged cheese sealed in wax, and corked bottles of purple and red juices.

"It may not be a feast, but I don't need much." She helped herself to a little bit of each thing and carried her lunch to a low table. She set out her food and settled on the bench to eat. She pulled her book out from the back of her dress and read while she ate, one of her favorite things to do when she ate alone.

This book contained a simple story of a lost man and a kind woman who found love and family with each other. It was her favorite. It always left her feeling hopeful for her future.

Her thoughts turned to her family. Her younger sisters could be quite chatty sometimes, and her brothers had plenty to say. Most of the time she enjoyed the constant conversation, but sometimes it was a bit much. She should enjoy the chance to read in peace.

But today, she couldn't focus on the book. Her heart ached for her family. For her people. She hoped they would be safe until she returned. With the rain. For she wouldn't go back without it.

Then her mind turned to Kian. If this didn't work the way she needed it to, she would marry not for love, but for the well-being of her family. Another reason to stick this out until she got what she came for.

Indira tidied up her plate and washed out her cup. She wiped down the surface of the table to clean up any wayward crumbs. It left bright streaks on the dusty surface.

"This place could use a good cleaning. In fact, the whole castle could!"

Maybe that would convince the Guardian that she planned to stay. If she started cleaning the whole place up like she planned to live there forever. She smirked to herself.

"Challenge accepted."

She gathered cleaning supplies from some shelves on one side of the kitchen and carried a bucket of water, scrub brushes, a broom, and a duster on a long pole with her.

"No better place to start than the beginning!" She hummed a cheerful tune while she cleaned the entry hall of the palace.

She used the long-handled duster to reach as high as she could to remove the cobwebs in the corners. She couldn't reach the chandelier. Maybe she'd find a ladder or something later on that would help her clean it. For now, it would have to wait.

She dusted the banister of the stairway. She swept up the dirt and shooed the fluffy dust bunnies huddled in the corners out the door.

Next, she dipped the scrub brush into her water bucket and crawled along the floor. She scrubbed every last bit of it until her back ached and her arms begged her to stop. She sat up and looked around.

"Not bad work, Indi!" Her cheerful voice echoed through the grand entry.

A door slammed on the fourth floor.

She gazed at the high ceiling. "You're welcome!" she hollered.

She picked herself up and carefully returned to the door to inspect her handiwork.

"Time to clean up my cleaning supplies!" She giggled at her own joke. She returned the items to the kitchen and carried a dustpan filled with the debris outside to empty. Right when she crossed the threshold, her foot caught on an exterior step. The dustpan jerked in her hand. The dust flew into the air and fell to the ground like snow.

The dust made her sneeze several times, which dislodged more dust from her clothes, which made her sneeze even more. She doubled over from the force of the sneezes. Two fingers pinched her nose to prevent herself from sneezing again.

Had the Guardian been spying on her, he would have seen the whole fiasco. But he had slammed the door to his suite. He was still tucked away from view. At least, that's what Indira told herself.

At least an empty castle meant no one would witness her regular clumsiness. Something else to add to her list of positive aspects of this endeavor.

"A walk through the garden should clear my nose." She untied the apron she had found in the kitchen from around her waist, set it on the bottom step, and wandered through the garden behind the library.

Paths paved with large flat stones wound their way between flower beds and low hedges. Some of the pathways curved in gentle turns around circular gardens. The plantings had been arranged with the tallest flowering plants in the center and shorter plants and flowers layered to the edges.

Other paths turned at right angles around the corners of precisely trimmed hedges. Within the low hedges stood taller evergreen shrubs and trees that had been cut to resemble animals of every kind. They reminded Indira of the statues in the front of the palace, but without the ominous feeling of real people frozen in time.

A slow-moving stream babbled its way through another part of the garden. Its source may not be readily apparent, but it provided a peaceful ambiance that Indira relished.

The trail led to an arched footbridge with high railings. Indira stood at the crest and gazed at her colorful surroundings. Birds chirped in the trees and shrubs. Butterflies and bees flitted from blossom to blossom. This would be a wonderful place to read when she needed a break from… whatever else she decided to do to convince the Guardian to help her.

She tipped her head back and looked at the rear of the palace. Tall windows lined the Guardian's wing of the fourth floor. All the curtains were drawn, and the sunlight and blue sky reflected off the glass windows. What did he do in there all day, every day, for years and years?

Suppertime approached after Indira's long stroll through the vast garden. Hopefully her bag that she had left in the parlor would still hold the food she had saved, and not mysteriously disappeared like her muffins.

When she arrived in the parlor where she had left her things, her bag was indeed empty of all food. But it didn't matter, for the sideboard had been restocked with another enticing feast! Enough to feed her entire family, even though Indira only needed food for one.

Did the Guardian supply this for her? That didn't make sense if he was so insistent that she leave. Perhaps he provided it as encouragement to gather what she could to take home and share with her people? She mulled this over while she ate fresh fruit and vegetables with savory dips, crackers and jellies, warm bread and melty butter, and enough roast beef that it would take her days and days to eat it all.

When she had eaten enough to satisfy her hunger, and perhaps a smidge more, she reclined on the sofa and read a book she had borrowed from the palace library. A fairytale about pixies and pegasus and other magical creatures.

Sometime later she awoke to a scraping sound from the entry way. The book lay open across her chest and a little bit of drool dripped from the side of her open mouth.

Her sleeve acted as a handkerchief to hastily wipe her face, then she stood to investigate the source of the sound. Her footsteps across the carpeted floor were quiet as a mouse. She paused in the doorway to the parlor.

A trail of ice followed the path of the Guardian. He pushed one of the circular tables to a different spot, returning it to the right place after Indi had moved it for cleaning. She hurried back to the sofa before he spotted her.

A few moments later he appeared in the doorway.

A cool breeze blew her way with his appearance.

She acted surprised to see him but didn't rise from her relaxed position on the sofa with her borrowed book open in front of her.

"You're still here." The Guardian stated the fact instead of asking the question. As if he hadn't already known with all the work and noise she had made that day. He had finished repositioning the furniture! Not only had the cleaning been noisy, but the singing and humming and talking to herself had carried to the fourth floor, she was sure.

"Yep," she answered with a sweet, sincere smile.

"I can make you go," he reminded her. He had his strange, feathered arms folded across his chest. His words fogged the air. Frost radiated on the floor from beneath his hooves.

She felt his will press against her mind. She didn't flinch. "I'll keep coming back if you do."

He grumbled deep within his massive chest and left without another word.

"Progress!" she whispered.

Eleven

Kian followed her through the village like one of the children asking for treats or a story. He talked and talked about himself and his wealth and his enormous house and how happy they were together now that they were wed.

Indira hurried her steps. She tried to walk faster than he could keep up while he droned on and on. It didn't work, of course. His legs were so much longer than hers. The top of her head barely reached his chest.

She tuned out his words and made her way through the town. The people looked healthy and happy. The landscape was green and fertile. She found herself in front of Kian's "enormous" house and he sidled up beside her. He wrapped his arms around her waist *from behind and kissed her neck.*

She squirmed beneath his touch and pulled away.

What was this? She was married to him? It couldn't be. Was that the only way to save her people? But how? It's not like Kian could bring back the rain!

She started to hyperventilate. She sank to the ground and closed her eyes. Tried to steady her breathing and calm herself.

Kian's voice faded and the smells and sounds of the castle garden filled her senses instead.

When she opened her eyes, her village and Kian were gone. She was in the castle garden. She breathed a sigh of relief.

She pulled herself to her feet and was about to stroll through the pristine garden.

"Hello," a male voice said behind her.

She inwardly groaned. Was Kian at the castle now, too? She turned, fully expecting to see his messy dark hair, perfect dimpled face, and lovey-dovey eyes pinned on her.

But someone entirely different stood in the garden with her, instead.

This man had wavy hair the color of glowing embers in a dying fire. His face was pale and flecked with more of the same coppery color. Instead of brown eyes like Kian's and her own, his eyes were the same blue as a perfect summer sky.

She swallowed.

He was a bit shorter than Kian. If she stood beside him, she would be at eye level with his chin instead of his chest. And he was not quite as broad across the shoulders as Kian, either. But even beneath his loose white shirt and tight tan pants she could see that he was well built. His shirt was unbuttoned at the top and she could see his pale skin across his collarbones.

He was the opposite of Kian in every way possible. At least physically.

"It's nice to see you here." He spoke in a wary voice.

Indira didn't speak. This was obviously a dream.

She understood why she had dreamed about home. And about Kian, unfortunately. But she had never seen this man before in her life. Why was he in her dream? What was her subconscious trying to communicate to her by having him here?

Of course, perhaps her mind was trying to give her some relief from all the worries that she had pushed aside that day. And from visions of being stuck as Kian's little wife for the rest of her miserable life. Besides, she was doing everything she could to try to fix the problem back home. No sense in worrying until there was something specific to be worried about.

Well, here we are. A random guy in my dream. Should she engage with this figment of her imagination?

She shrugged. "Why not?"

She stepped forward and shook the man's hand firmly with her own. "Hi. I'm Indira. My friends call me Indi. It's great to meet you." Her words and manner were direct, something that her mother always scolded her for.

But her mother was not here, and this was a dream, after all, so why bend to societal pressure to be demure and ladylike if she didn't have to? She grinned at the thought.

The mystery-man's blue eyes stared back at her as if he didn't know what to say.

A step in his direction caused him to stiffen, but she looped her hand through the man's arm and motioned for him to lead her on a stroll through the garden.

"Tell me about your beautiful garden," she said in a casual tone.

He tensed. "How do you know this is my garden?" he asked with a slight frown.

"Because it's not my garden, so it must be yours. Go on, don't be shy!" She nudged him forward.

He stayed quiet for a minute as if deciding if he should play along.

Patience was not a struggle for her, so she continued her leisurely stroll while she waited for him to speak.

He nodded once and led her through the walkways. His voice was timid, but he was clearly familiar with the garden. He pointed several plants and flowers here and there. "I don't know a lot, only what I've read in the books from the library, but I believe the design is based on the gardens at the palace in the northlands."

Curious how Indira's mind had invented that fact. She didn't know anything about the palace in the northlands. Maybe that's why her mind had come up with that. She couldn't be wrong if they were made up facts!

Indira didn't act shy at all, like she normally would have if going on a stroll through a romantic garden, alone with a handsome young man. He wasn't real, so there was no point in being nervous.

"Do you know where these originated from?" she asked him as she inhaled the divine scent of an exotic-looking flower. Pale pink petals opened to reveal dazzling golden fronds pouring out of the center.

He shook his head and answered in a soft voice. "Tropical. Perhaps from the islands." He told her what he knew about them in simple, short answers.

At least the man her mind had paired her with wasn't full of himself like Kian!

Her new dream-man gave her a strange sideways look.

She distracted him with more questions about the garden. They inspected the variety of plants and insects. Indira scratched behind the ears of a cute little bunny that hopped across their path while her companion stood and watched with stiff, formal posture.

"She's so soft! You should try!" she smiled up at him.

His piercing blue eyes widened. He shook his head ever so slightly in refusal. Like he didn't think it would be appropriate behavior, or something.

By the time they reached the gurgling stream that Indira had seen in the real garden, she was confident that this was all a figment of her imagination.

"Come, sit by me," she invited after they crossed the miniature arched bridge over the water.

She settled herself on the soft grass beside the stream and let her fingers float in the water. A pair of dragonflies danced along the surface of the stream. An orange and white spotted fish swam in circles in the shade of the bridge.

The man stared at her. He seemed uncomfortable in her presence, even though he had been cordial during their time together. Perhaps he was uncomfortable with her relaxed behavior?

She rolled her eyes inwardly. This whole figment of her

imagination thing was becoming complicated.

After sitting without speaking for a long time, she broke the silence. "Well, this has been a very relaxing, um, afternoon." She looked at the sky to determine the time of day it was in the dream. It was difficult to tell. The light was bland and dull, but it definitely was not nighttime. "I hope you have a wonderful day. I'm going to wake up now."

She stood, closed her eyes, and told herself to wake up.

When she opened her eyes, she found herself in the black void of her original dream once more. The table with the hourglass stood in front of her. The sand had shifted so more sat at the bottom than what was left in the top.

She pinched her eyebrows together and reached for the hourglass. She would turn it over and start the time again.

She startled awake in the parlor.

Frustration burned the back of her throat. Why had she wasted so much time in the garden with some fictional man instead of going into the castle, finding the hourglass, and destroying it for good?

She threw herself back onto her pillow. She would sleep and dream again and do that. Then at least she wouldn't feel like time was running out. She didn't know what the end of the time would bring, but it couldn't be good.

She squeezed her eyes shut but it was no use. She was no longer tired. She sat up again and sighed. She would try again next time.

Even though the dream in the garden had been calm and relaxing, she didn't feel like she had slept very well. Her eyes were puffy and dry. Her usually present smile was missing. Her eyebrows pointed down instead and tension squeezed her head all the way around.

If she had been at home with her family, they would have joked that "Grumpy Indi" had joined them for breakfast and to stay out of her way. It always made her bad mood worse.

But now it made her miss her family. It spurred her into action.

She finished investigating the last few rooms on the ground floor of the palace before she got to work cleaning some more.

Each of the rooms were small. Some were guest rooms. One room had funny little puppet stages on one side and seats like a theater against the opposite wall.

The walls of another room were painted black and bright luminescent dots had been painted carefully on every surface. It looked like the night sky. She even recognized constellations. A telescopic looking glass sat in the center and pointed askew toward the floor. What good would that do inside a room *painted* to look like the sky? What was one supposed to see besides a close-up view of the strange dots on the walls and ceiling?

The last room was filled with plants and cages of all

shapes and sizes. The excess of greenery filled the room with humidity like she hadn't felt in ages. The moisture soaked into her skin. And probably turned her hair into a halo of frizz.

With the large leafy plants and moist moss-covered floor, it was like walking through a jungle!

Inside the cages Indira discovered such a variety of birds that she had never seen before. Rainbow birds with golden crests and long colorful tail feathers, doves with blue spots on their wings and striking blue eyes- kind of like that man from her dream! A miniature kingfisher with variegated blue and red feathers on its head and wings.

A striking sparrow that should have been brown but had iridescent purple feathers on its head and back blinked at her with its tiny black eyes. Another cage with a mother owl and a pair of owlets hung in one corner. Only these owls had rainbow feathers instead of white or tawny brown!

And there were a wide variety of songbirds that she recognized from her travels along the river.

The songs filled the space with a melody that seemed to be trying to tell her something. It felt serene. Almost romantic. Was it possible for birds to blend their voices into a tune like that? It was as if they performed for her.

The room felt bigger on the inside than it should have been because the walls were painted to look like a tropical forest with bright skies and beautiful flowers.

She could spend all day here! And who took care of these birds? The Guardian? She didn't think his wide shoulders and broad antlers would fit!

"This whole place is full of mysteries, isn't it?" she said to one of the colorful birds.

It looked at her and bobbed its head like it nodded yes.

She grinned, her bad mood behind her.

Now she could get to work on her plan to whittle the Guardian down into helping her even if it was to get rid of her.

She cleaned one of the sitting rooms, making sure to sing extra cheerfully and extra loud. She even propped the bird room door open so the birds could join her.

She removed all the furniture covers and folded them carefully. She would carry them to the kitchen later and wash them, hang them to dry, and find a cupboard to store them in. She arranged the books and knickknacks just so on the floating shelves on one wall. She found tall, wide candles to line up on the mantle over the fireplace. And she threw the deep burgundy curtains open to let in the sunlight. Probably for the first time in… what? Years? Decades?

How old was the Mountain Guardian? How long had he lived here? And why hadn't she thought of those questions before?

Tonight, she would ask him. Try to get to know him better. And if worse came to worst, she would talk about herself until she was blue in the face. It's hard to say no to someone you like. She had to get him to like her.

Twelve

When the Mountain Guardian came to the parlor that night to make his statement about her still being there, instead of telling him she was, which she knew he already knew, or challenging him even in a sweet voice, she asked her questions.

She stood in front of him and maintained eye contact while she wore a pleasant smile. She made sure to keep her shoulders relaxed and her hands at her sides.

"I love your home. How long have you lived here?"

He lifted his nose a little higher. One of his moose ears twitched.

Do you have a name? Were you born here, or did you come later in life?" She kept her smile the entire time.

He made a noise in his throat like he wasn't sure how to answer her questions.

"Who made all those magnificent pieces of art you have here? And where'd all the books come from? Are they yours?"

He stiffened. His eyes hardened. She didn't even think that was possible.

"Do you have family? Do they ever come to visit?" she tried again.

"Leave." He growled at her. He stormed from the room, leaving a trail of icy patches across the floor.

His heavy footsteps echoed through the hall and up the stairs. And once again the slam of a door announced his arrival to his personal quarters on the fourth floor.

"It was worth a try. Maybe he'll be more amenable to conversation tomorrow. Speaking of which…"

She was very much looking forward to sleep that night. She would find the hourglass, destroy it, and buy her village some time. At least, that's what she thought it would do. It couldn't hurt to try.

"If only the room was just a smidge warmer…" she said out loud as she settled on the sofa.

The fire brightened a bit. She snuggled into the pillows and blankets and basked in its warmth. She intentionally relaxed each part of her body from head to toe. She focused on her breathing so that she would fall asleep quickly.

Her breathing slowed. She felt herself drift to sleep.

She stood in the middle of the garden again.

"Perfect!" she breathed.

"Hello," the copper-haired man said from behind her. His tone reflected his uncertainty at her presence.

"Hi. I have some things I need to do. See you later!" She waved at him and rushed toward the library doors at the back of the castle.

"Wait! Where are you going!" the man called after her. He quickly caught up to her.

Darn these short legs! Here we go again, she said to herself.

The man placed a gentle hand on her arm. Not possessive and controlling like Kian always did when he wanted her to stop. More like an invitation that she could heed if she wanted to.

She paused and looked up into his cornflower-blue eyes. "Yes?" she asked in a sincerely curious tone.

"Please." He looked up at the castle with a worried expression. "I don't think you should go in there." His voice was rough with concern.

She looked at the glass door of the library. "Why not?" The hourglass was just on the other side. She really really wanted to smash it.

The man glanced at the castle again, and she saw that his eyes settled much higher than the library windows. What was he looking at?

She followed his gaze with her own. The shadowy form of the Mountain Guardian loomed in one of the tall windows on the fourth floor.

His antlers moved as he pivoted his head. His dark eyes met hers. He yanked the curtains closed and disappeared from her view.

"Why shouldn't I go in the castle?" she asked absentmindedly, not taking her eyes off that window.

"I... I don't think it's safe," the man pleaded.

She returned her eyes to his.

When her brown eyes met his blue ones, his eyes widened. The fear in his eyes softened. His gaze held wonder, like he hadn't ever locked eyes with a woman before.

Her heart skipped a beat.

Maybe if Kian tried looking at her like that, she might melt under his gaze the way he wanted her to.

She blinked. What was she thinking? She needed to destroy the hourglass.

"I think it's fine. I've met... him." She gestured at the upper window. "I'm not afraid of him."

The man dropped his hand from her arm. "You're not?" He sounded confused.

"No. If he wanted to hurt me, he would have done it by now. He looks intimidating, but I don't think he is bad." She paused. "Why? Do you have a different experience with him?" She tipped her head to one side.

The man shook his head slowly. "No. It's just, usually when people see a creature like that, they assume the worst. I just thought, I mean. I assumed the worst, too. He looks like a beast. Why wouldn't he act like one?"

Indira looked longingly toward the library. Then she looked at this man again. He looked lost and confused. Her heart softened for him.

"What's your name?" she asked him as she settled on a stone bench nearby.

He sat beside her but left as much space between them as the bench would allow.

He frowned. "You can call me Dev."

"Great. Dev, some people may look like monsters on the outside."

Dev flinched at her words.

She paused. Was she being too outspoken again?

He didn't say anything, so she continued.

"But even those who appear… brutish… on the outside can be good people on the inside."

Dev didn't react to her words.

"On the other hand, some people are tremendously appealing in their appearance." Her eyes roved over his handsome features. His cheeks reddened in a deep blush. "But turn out to be beasts on the inside." She thought of Kian when she said this part.

Dev leaned forward with wide, sad eyes. "I'm not a monster," he whispered.

"No! Dev, of course not. That's not what I was implying at all." She touched her hand to her forehead and closed her eyes. "I'm just saying, you can't always judge someone by their appearance, you know? You have to get to know a person before you decide if they are good or not." She rested a hand on his arm.

He shivered slightly.

It would seem that her social unease carried over into her dreams, as well. She removed her hand from his arm and folded hers both into her lap.

"I believe this to be true as well." Dev's eyes were downcast. He kept his voice quiet.

Tension hung in the air between them. She couldn't tell if it was good tension or bad tension. Either way she wanted Dev to feel comfortable with her.

"Take a walk with me?" She rose and extended a hand toward him.

He looked up at her. His dark copper eyelashes contrasted with his bright blue eyes. He took her hand and stood.

"You choose which way," she encouraged him with a warm smile.

He led her on a quiet stroll through the garden, her hand nestled in the crook of his arm. It probably should have been uncomfortable since they barely knew each other, but since it was a dream…

Indira walked beside Dev in pleasant silence. The hourglass remained forgotten.

Indira's eyes opened slowly. She hadn't wanted the dream to end. Dev was easy to be with, even if he didn't talk much. And he wasn't unpleasant to look at, either.

"Indira!" she scolded herself. "He's a figment of your imagination. Stop swooning over him! You have more important things to do anyway!"

She spent another day cleaning, loudly singing, and trying to enjoy herself to distract herself from worrying about her home and family.

The Mountain Guardian growled the same statement to her at the end of the day. "You're still here."

She ignored his statement and asked, "What kinds of books do you like to read?"

Without answering he left her in a blast of cold air. Again.

Dev greeted her in the garden. His face held a shy smile this time.

"That smile looks good on you," she commented when she approached him. She slipped her hand into the crook of his arm.

His face turned crimson, and the smile disappeared.

She could get it back. Did he have a dimple in his cheeks, like Kian? She was so focused on trying to get Dev to smile in order to find out, that she all but forgot about the hourglass.

"Do you come from a large family?" she asked him.

He murmured an unintelligible reply then asked, "Do you?"

"Oh yes!" She waved her free hand in the air. "I have six siblings and two amazing parents." She told him about her father's once thriving shipping business, and about the hungry children in her town. Her voice filled the air for nearly a quarter of an hour!

"Now your turn," she teased. "What kinds of things did you enjoy doing when you were a child?"

He furrowed his brow and rubbed his chin. "Let me think…" he said quietly. "Tell me about yours while I decide?"

Without skipping a beat, Indira spilled the details about the mischief she managed when she was young. She told him about how difficult it was to be the oldest child, how her parents burdened her with a lot of responsibility, but that she loved her family and would do anything for them.

Her words wandered away from memories of when she was young and turned to the current predicament of her village.

"We haven't had rain in ages. The land has dried up. I'm here to get the Mountain Guardian to help me. When the rains return and our village is green again, I will petition my father to apprentice on one of his sailing vessels. He'll say no, of course, but I can wear him down, I'm sure."

Indira's daydreams about captaining a sea vessel did the trick. Or maybe it was the lively way in which she imagined riding the ship through a storm, and yelling commands to her crew.

Just as she had hoped, the excitement in her voice and in her demeanor had pulled that hidden smile back out of Dev and planted it right back onto his face.

She knew better than to comment on it, but her heart felt light seeing it there again.

Near the end of their walk, Dev asked her a new question. "What sorts of books do you like to read?"

She glanced at him from the corner of her eye. "Where did that question come from?" she teased. Afterall, she had been the one asking the questions.

He stumbled over his words. "You are always glancing at the library… I just thought you liked books," he said in a hurry.

The library! She groaned inwardly. She meant to get her hands on that hourglass, but Dev's bright smile upon her arrival had distracted her completely.

"Are you alright?" Dev asked her with a concerned look. His smile had disappeared again.

She glanced at the library. Apparently, she did that a lot. She guessed the hourglass could wait. Maybe she'd be able to convince the Guardian to help her the next day.

She nodded and grinned at Dev, which elicited a new smile from him.

She relaxed. "I do! I love all kinds of books. Adventurous tales, romantic relationships, anything that takes me away for a little bit, you know?"

Dev hadn't taken his eyes off of her face as she spoke. His eyes softened around the edges. His cheeks flushed, but not deep crimson like earlier.

She placed a hand on her stomach to still the butterflies that danced inside.

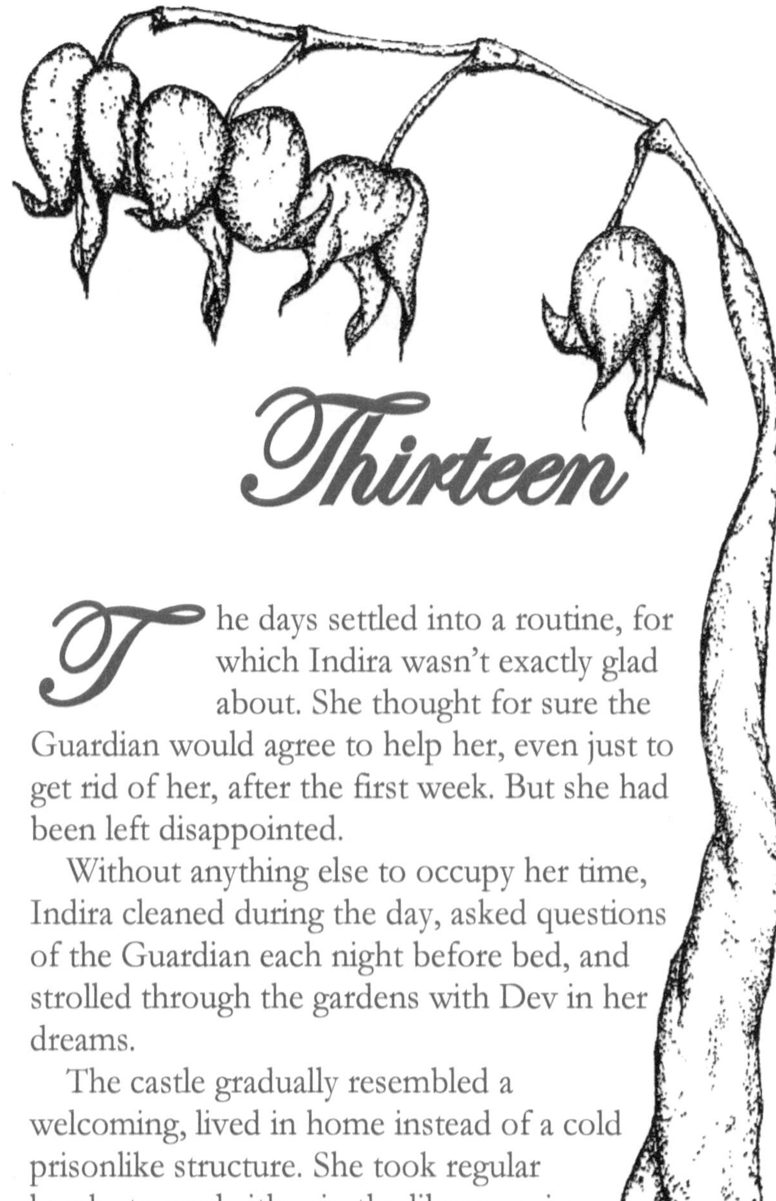

Thirteen

The days settled into a routine, for which Indira wasn't exactly glad about. She thought for sure the Guardian would agree to help her, even just to get rid of her, after the first week. But she had been left disappointed.

Without anything else to occupy her time, Indira cleaned during the day, asked questions of the Guardian each night before bed, and strolled through the gardens with Dev in her dreams.

The castle gradually resembled a welcoming, lived in home instead of a cold prisonlike structure. She took regular breaks to read either in the library or in one of the gardens outside the castle.

The Guardian approached her each night and told her to leave, to which she answered in the negative each and every time. She pestered him with questions, which he did not answer. "What is your favorite food?" "Do you like being outdoors?" "Do you have any plans for the future?" He only grumbled complaints about her continued presence. When she asked him about his family or memories from his past, his mood turned sour. Or rather, more sour than his usual mood.

The hourglass no longer haunted her dreams. She abandoned the idea of smashing it altogether. It probably wouldn't make a difference anyway. If it came up in her dreams again, she would take care of it.

In the meantime, she would enjoy her nightly garden outings with Dev. She didn't understand the purpose of the dreams with Dev, but it helped her sort through her worries for her family and her feelings about being at the Mountain Guardian's castle.

"You know you can leave any time, right? He is not holding you captive," Dev reminded her in a solemn tone.

"Of course. But I vowed I would not leave until he helps my people," Indira stated matter-of-factly.

"But don't you miss your family?" Dev questioned. His look was so serious.

"More than anything." She paused and pictured her family back at home. "But if I return with nothing, then this whole

journey, all this time away, will have been for nothing. I came here to find a way to save them. And I believe he," she gestured toward the castle, "can help."

"How can you be so certain?" Dev furrowed his brow. "What if he can't help you?"

Indira stopped her steps. She turned to look at Dev. He rarely questioned her like this. He normally stayed quiet and allowed her to do most of the talking. Where his voice and manner were usually timid, he suddenly behaved as if he carried a heavy load.

"I don't know." She held his gaze. "But something in my gut tells me he can. Don't you ever believe something to be true so much that you find that it is?"

Dev looked away. "That takes an awful lot of effort. And can lead to massive disappointment."

She reached up and gently pulled his face back to meet her eyes again. "But it can also change your life. Change the world. Isn't that risk worth taking sometimes?"

He stared into her eyes for several long moments, then backed away a step from her and cleared his throat. He blinked and looked away.

She dropped her hand from his cheek and stiffened. She had felt something between them in that moment. Her heart fluttered and she felt a little weak at the knees. Had he felt it to? Is that why he had moved away so suddenly?

She dropped her gaze. She shouldn't let her heart get caught up in… whatever this thing with Dev was. What was it, anyway? A recurring dream?

Dev stepped along the path. He turned a corner to continue their stroll. He didn't look back.

Had she said something wrong? Was it possible to offend someone who wasn't even real?

Indira awoke feeling very confused.

The Mountain Guardian's presence grew less rigid each night when he confronted her. He began *asking* her if she would leave instead of gruffly commanding her to. His footsteps no longer brought frost with him through the castle. His posture relaxed ever so slightly.

He still refused to answer any of her questions. He still refused to offer her the relief for her people that she so desperately needed. But as the days passed, he seemed sorry to say no, instead of angry.

As the dreams continued, Dev relaxed more in Indira's presence. She still did most of the talking, as usual, but he smiled more often, joined in her laughter from time to time, and allowed himself to react with emotion to her stories.

But whenever Indira asked him questions about himself, he always deferred the conversation back to her.

It made Indira uneasy. Was there something he was hiding from her?

"Why do you avoid my questions?" She finally blurted when he did it again.

His smile disappeared, which pricked at Indi's heart. But she needed to know.

"I am sorry," he replied so quietly she almost couldn't hear.

His voice sounded tight. He had a pained look on his face, in his eyes.

"I'm sorry, Dev," Indi hurried to say. "I didn't mean to offend you. It's just, I have told you pretty much everything about me that there is to know!" she let out a self-deprecating laugh. Again, with the social awkwardness. She shook the thought away.

Dev nodded. "I know, Indi. I am sorry for not being forthcoming with you."

Indira braced herself for whatever he was about to say. Would she be left disappointed?

It's a dream, Indi, her mind shouted. She ignored it.

"I am afraid I do not remember anything about my past. Or how I came to be here. All I know is that I wander this garden each night while that thing watches."

It was not what Indira expected to hear. At all.

"Dev, I'm sorry…" she started to say.

He held out a hand to stop her apology. The dark tone of his next words left Indira unsettled.

"I wish I could destroy the Guardian."

"What?" she whispered.

A tear dripped down one of his cheeks. "I am a prisoner here. I wish to be free of this place. Of him." A sob escaped his throat. He turned away from her.

All unease melted away. She rushed to his side and turned him to face her. Then she threw her arms around his torso. She squeezed him tight.

He didn't immediately return the embrace. She didn't let go. After several long moments, he finally allowed his arms to *encircle her.*

"I am so sorry, Dev." She spoke against his shoulder. "I will find a way to help you, too. I promise."

He didn't respond, just leaned into her, and nodded.

The following night Indira confronted the Guardian. "Do you keep prisoners in your dungeon?" She lifted her nose to try to make herself feel brave. But her heart raced wildly in her chest.

How would he react to her accusations? And if he did keep prisoners, was she sentencing herself to join the others by asking?

The Guardian gave her a shocked look. His expression was hard to read on his inhuman face, but she thought she saw hurt in his strange eyes.

She softened. "I've heard rumors, is all…" she said in a milder tone.

He glared down his nose at her. "You should leave."

He turned on his hooves and stormed away again. Much like he had done when she first arrived.

"Now you've done it, Indi. You've offended him. Just when you thought you might be making progress." She groaned and threw herself onto the sofa.

She had promised Dev she did not consider the Guardian a monster, and then she had accused him of keeping prisoners. Like a monster. What was wrong with her?

She did not dream of Dev that night. She only dreamt of the hourglass slowly running out of time with no way of stopping it.

At the end of the following day, Indira's thirteenth day in the castle, she found a gift on the table beside her sofa in the parlor.

A rectangle wrapped in soft, silky purple cloth and tied with a lacey black ribbon.

She looked around the room. The supper was ready for her on the sideboard. But everything else was exactly how she had left it that morning.

She picked up the package and sank into the couch. She carefully tugged on the ribbon and let it fall onto her lap. She rested the rectangle on her thighs and peeled away the silky fabric.

She gasped. A gorgeous book of poems and sonnets lay before her. The gilded page edges sparkled in the firelight. The embossed designs on the leather cover tickled her fingers as she caressed them. The scent of a well-loved book reached her nose.

The Mountain Guardian appeared in the doorway. She turned to look at him.

He didn't give her a command. He didn't ask her to leave. He looked at her and asked, "Do you like it?"

She could only nod. Her heart raced. He had given this gift to her?

"Thank you," she answered in a quiet voice.

He nodded once then turned to leave.

She jumped from the couch and ran to the doorway.

She held on to the door jam with both hands.

"Guardian!"

He paused and turned his head slightly, his moose ear pricked in her direction.

"Why?" She couldn't think of how to ask without sounding rude. No other words came out of her mouth.

He let out a slow breath. He didn't answer.

She watched him make his way slowly up the stairs and out of sight.

She returned to the sofa. She held the book in her arms as she drifted to sleep.

Home, the way it once was, filled her dreams and heart with a promise of hope.

She awoke just before dawn to whispers behind the sofa. She opened her eyes very slowly. As quiet as she could, she lifted herself against the back of the sofa to discover the source of the whispers.

She sucked in a sharp breath.

The whispering halted. Two heads atop small bodies turned very slowly toward her. Two sets of round brown eyes locked onto hers. They stood as still as statues.

She waited for them to do or say something.

They didn't move a muscle.

She was afraid of startling them, so she stayed still, too.

Suddenly, one of the tiny people with long pointed ears yelled, "Enjoy your breakfast!" They sprinted out the door and out of sight.

She collapsed onto the couch. She had believed the Guardian to live alone. But he had two brownies at his service in the palace. How had he managed that? What could he possibly have to offer them in exchange for their service?

Another question for the Guardian. Since he hadn't been the one feeding her, he must know about these tiny men delivering her food on a daily basis. If he hadn't specifically asked her about the book, she might have thought they were responsible for that, too. But that had been a gift from the Guardian himself.

After another long day of cleaning, she waited for the Guardian to arrive so she could ask him about the food-delivery-creatures. Or whatever they were.

Instead of the Guardian coming and asking her politely to leave, and she politely refusing, a note slid underneath the door that stood slightly ajar.

She picked it up and unfolded the thick parchment.

"You should stay in the queen's suite on the fourth floor," she read out loud.

She flipped the parchment over. There was no signature. No indication of who had written it. It wasn't an invitation, exactly, but a suggestion.

Was it from the Guardian? Why wouldn't he ask her?

Or was it from those little men? Was it a trick of some kind?

She opened the door to attempt to discover the sender, but the entryway was as empty as always.

Fourteen

"Dev!" Relief overwhelmed Indira when the garden, and Dev, returned to her dream that night. She didn't fully understand why. Maybe because she needed someone to talk to. She poured her thoughts out and Dev listened, as usual.

"I messed things up with the Guardian." She plopped onto the soft mossy ground, propped her elbows on her folded knees, and rested her chin in her hands. "I'm such a fool!" She groaned.

Dev lowered himself to sit beside her. He wasn't stiff and formal like when they had first met. He stretched his legs in front of him and propped himself on his hands behind him. He didn't interrupt.

"I asked him about keeping prisoners! Why did I do that? I've been making progress,

129

wearing him down so he will help me."

Dev's laughter rang through the garden.

Indira straightened from her slouch and gave him an affronted look. "Why are you laughing at me?"

"I'm sure you haven't ruined anything." He suppressed more laughter.

She stared at him. "That doesn't explain the laughing," she asserted.

"I am sorry, Indi. You look so cute all put out." He mimicked a pouting face.

"I do not look like that!" she countered firmly.

He laughed again. "Except you do! It's adorable, I promise!" He reached toward her.

She dodged his touch. "This isn't funny! I need the Guardian's help. Otherwise I'll be stuck here forever!" She fell backwards onto the moss and stretched flat on the ground.

When Dev didn't respond, didn't react at all she propped herself on one elbow to discover why.

He had a troubled expression on his face.

"What did I say wrong this time?" She moaned and fell to the ground again. Covered her face with her hands. She couldn't win. Even with a fictional person she put her foot in her mouth over and over again.

A warm hand touched her arm.

She lowered her arms and peered at Dev. He looked really upset now.

"Now I've ruined things with you, too." She sat up and sighed.

Dev rested a hand on her arm. Her skin tingled beneath his touch. *"You haven't ruined anything, Indi."*

"Your pinched eyebrows and turned down lips suggest otherwise," she pointed out.

He pulled his hand away and ran his fingers through this hair. He dragged both hands down the sides of his face. *"Indira, what if the Guardian can't help you? What will you do then?"* He spoke as if he chose his words very carefully.

"I don't know. I haven't thought that far ahead. He's real, he's here, he seems to have some control over the elements, from what I can gather. He'll help me." She shrugged and jutted her chin out.

Dev touched her chin with a single finger. He had a sad look in his eyes. *"But what if..."*

"Nope. No what ifs. I don't accept failure as an option. He will help me, or I'll die waiting."

Dev dropped his hand and closed his eyes.

"Let's talk about something else." Indira leapt to her feet. *"I have a dilemma."*

"Another one?" Dev's sarcasm seemed forced, but Indi pretended not to notice.

She told him all about the gift the Guardian had left for her that day.

"See? Told you he wasn't angry with you..."

Indira shushed him and he pinched his lips together. A little bit of mirth returned to his eyes.

"Then I got this note that said I should move into the queen's suite on the fourth floor!" She gave him an exasperated look.

He didn't react.

"Well?" She prodded.

"Well, what? Are you going to do it?" Dev asked in a matter-of-fact way.

"What if it's a trick? And the Guardian gets really angry. Again! He could throw me out of the castle! Or lock me in the dungeon! Or turn me into a frozen statue!" She listed the unlikely but very real possibilities.

Dev grinned at her and shook his head. "A frozen statue?" He sounded amused.

She didn't explain. Just stared at him with nervous eyes.

"Right. Does anyone use those rooms?" He schooled his features.

"Well, no." Her lowered eyebrows expressed her confusion at the situation.

"Do they look like they are special to him in any way?" he prodded.

"No. In fact the doors are too small for him to even enter any of them."

"You should do it. Give him the benefit of the doubt. You've said before you are not afraid of him…"

"I'm not afraid he's going to hurt me. I really need him to help me. And I can't get him to do that if I'm locked in a dungeon or banished forever."

Dev laughed. "I doubt he'll banish you. You've brought so much life and light to the palace!" He glanced at her sideways as if he hadn't meant to say that.

She pretended not to notice. "Alright." She decided. "I will do it. I will move into the queen's suite in the morning."

He reached for her hand and gave it a quick squeeze.

Her face warmed, but he probably couldn't see her blush

beneath her darker skin.

He didn't let go of her hand as they finished their stroll.

"I will see you tomorrow," he looked into her eyes when they reached the end of the path.

Her heart fluttered beneath his gaze. Why couldn't he be real, instead of a dream?

Indira didn't have anything to take with her to the rooms on the fourth floor. She bundled her old clothing into her satchel with her two books- the one from home and the gift from the Guardian. She allowed her eyes to wander around the parlor. It had become a cozy guest room in her two weeks at the palace. A little part of her would miss it!

But she squared her shoulders and told herself that she was doing the right thing. She marched across the now pristine entrance hall and up the wide, dust-free stairs. Then up the next two flights. She hadn't started cleaning the second floor yet. It desperately needed it, though. She made a mental list of what needed to be accomplished first.

At the top of the stairs on the fourth floor, Indira paused. She turned her head to glance to her left. Where the Mountain Guardian stayed. Did he know she was there, wondering about him? Would he be angry that she had assumed she was welcome to stay in the rooms on the opposite wing of the castle as his?

Her heart beat a little faster. Should she... ask him? She frowned and shook her head. She should trust

Dev and do it.

A strange thought came to her. If Dev was all in her head, how was she developing feelings for him?

She turned and took soft steps toward the women's rooms as her mind processed her thoughts.

Dev was not a person she had met before. She had seen people with his hair color and complexion on some of her travels but didn't know in what part of the land they made their home.

She entered the sitting room of the queen's wing. A fireplace took up one corner and a pair of wingback chairs, a settee, and a low table were arranged in a semicircle in front of the mantle. It was very cozy!

She especially loved the floral and paisley upholstery on the furniture. She ran her hand over the back of one of the chairs to feel the individual threads beneath her fingers. The color scheme in this space was all golds and pinks. Very welcoming. Very feminine.

A second door stood opposite the entrance to the hall outside. She pushed it open.

Inside the next chamber was a small table with two chairs for dining. A lower table with a bowl of fresh flowers arranged in the center. A two-person sofa for intimate conversations and taking tea with a guest. A guest like Dev.

She told herself to knock it off and keep moving through the suite.

The next part of the suite was divided into three separate rooms. A washroom with a vanity and porcelain tub. A huge closet filled with clothing that all seemed to be exactly her size. And a sleeping chamber with a massive four posted canopy bed laden with more squishy pillows and soft blankets than Indira knew existed. A huge bouquet of roses stood in a vase on the bedside table. They filled the room with a familiar floral scent that she first remembered experiencing in a dream.

Just like she had observed the first time she examined this space, the Guardian would not fit through any of the doors, even if he wanted to. And everything had been recently tidied, the windows washed, and the bedding fluffed.

Was that the work of the brownies, too? It must have been since it couldn't have been the Guardian.

Indira set her bag on the bed and sat on the edge. She bounced from the springiness of the mattress. She would definitely sleep well that night! Which reminded her of Dev. Again.

She had heard tales of people who had dreams that were different than regular dreams. They were real. Or something. She didn't fully understand.

Was it possible that Dev *was* a real person? One of those elusive Dreamers? And he had somehow entered her dreams? The thought made her blush. If he was real, then the feelings she developed for him could blossom into something more.

She scolded herself. "Now is not the time to be thinking of such things, Indi. You have much more important things to worry about now."

She told herself to focus on what needed to be done here. Now. Not in her dreams with a mysterious man that could be real, but was more likely a figment of her imagination, created by her mind to make her days here less lonely.

Even though the Mountain Guardian had softened somewhat, he mostly avoided her. She caught him watching her from a window, or an indoor balcony, or catwalk from the fourth floor from time to time. She always pretended not to notice. Instead, she would continue her humming and cleaning and making the space feel like a warm home instead of an icy palace.

If his melting toward her was any indication, she was sure she could convince him to help her people. She wasn't sure how much longer it would take.

She spent the afternoon organizing and cataloguing her new temporary living space. A bookshelf lined one wall of the room beyond the room with the bed. Several comfortable reading chairs faced the large windows on the back wall. The windows looked out over the garden where she spent her dreams with Dev.

She tried to settle in and peruse one of the books from the shelf, but whenever she saw movement outside, she couldn't help her eyes from darting to spot Dev.

She reminded herself that he wasn't real. Or, if he was real, he would only appear in her dreams. But perhaps if he was real, and he was familiar with this place, maybe he would show up one day?

She forced herself to push those thoughts aside. They would only lead to heartache and disappointment.

She shut the book, replaced it on the shelf, and prepared herself to return to the first floor to tidy up something else, instead. Preferably something that didn't face the garden behind the castle.

Instead of Dev greeting her in her dreams, like she hoped and expected, she found herself in the dark room. Alone. A light shone from some mystery lantern or something above. It illuminated the round table. And reflected off the smooth glass of the hourglass.

Three fourths of the sand now rested on the bottom. There wasn't very much left in the top. Her heart ached in her chest. Her legs shook. Was her time running out? What would happen if the sand all made it to the bottom before she could convince the Mountain Guardian to help her?

She cried out into the darkness. "Guardian! Please! You must help me!" Tears dripped down her cheeks.

There was no reply. Nothing but silence surrounded her.

"Mistress Mena," she whispered. "Why did you send me here if it was to lead to this? There must be something different I must do!"

She sunk to the hard, smooth floor. She could feel wood grain beneath her hand. Was she in the palace library? Was this the same table and hourglass that sat there now?

Instead of trying to break it in her dreams, what would happen if she were to smash it for real?

She woke up, threw the soft, downy blanket off her, and hurried down all the flights of stairs in her bare feet.

Her pale, thin, sleeveless nightgown brushed the floor and sent a chill up her arms and back. The shadows of the sconces, tables, and floral arrangements that had begun to appear throughout the castle since her arrival loomed surreal in the darkness. She hugged her arms with her hands, not just from the chill but also from the eeriness of the castle at night.

She hurried toward the library. She pushed the double doors open and barreled toward the table with the hourglass.

The other knickknacks stood in place. But the hourglass was missing. She frantically searched all the other shelves, tables, and mantles. She couldn't find it anywhere.

She roared in frustration. Now who sounded like a menacing beast? She sunk onto one of the sofas and rested her head in her hands. Tears, real ones, not the ones from her dreamland, melted down her face. She felt so stuck!

She wrapped one of the cozy reading blankets around herself in the tall wingback chair at one end of the library. She curled into a ball and stared out the window.

Moonlight illuminated the garden instead of the usual unchanging daylight of her dreams. Shadows of moths, bats, and other nocturnal flying creatures danced above the plants and pathways. Everything glowed with a strange blueness.

Her eyelids grew heavy as her mind turned in circles around worry, frustration, and fear.

Fifteen

You seem troubled tonight, Indi." Dev looked over at her with concern in his eyes. "Are you worried about home?" His words were laced with a hint of guilt.

She looked at him from the corner of her eye. "I am worried. And a bit frustrated that the Guardian refuses to help me." Indira sighed.

She shook her head. Should she tell him about Mistress Mena? If he was a real person, maybe he would know what to do. But if he was all in her head, then what was the point?

And of course, she was frustrated. If the Guardian could help, why did he refuse? What was he so afraid would happen to him if he helped her people?

Dev nodded as if he could hear her thoughts. Since he was all in her head anyway, perhaps he could.

"I'll be fine," she waved away her previous words- or thoughts- of complaint. But her head ached.

"I wish there was more I could do to help." Dev's words surprised Indi. As did his next action. He sent a threatening glare toward the fourth-floor window of the castle. His jaw muscles flexed as he ground his teeth. His utter contempt for the Guardian rolled off him in waves.

His hatred for the Guardian caught Indira off guard. She gasped as a thought entered her head. Would he harm the Guardian if he could?

Her heart rate increased, and her palms became clammy.

Why did the thought of Dev harming the Guardian upset her? Was it because it showed a dark side to Dev that she wanted to brush aside? Was it because she needed the Guardian to help her people? It must be the latter, she decided.

"Without the Guardian my people will suffer. As much as you loathe him, I need him whole. He has done nothing to harm me. Or you for that matter," she pointed out as gently as possible.

His eyes caressed her face. "I know that, Indi. That's what makes this whole situation so impossible." He wanted to say something more, but hesitated.

She held her breath.

He cleared his throat. He opened his mouth as if to speak. To tell her whatever his secret was. That he was not a figment of her imagination? That he was real? That he was a Dreamer, like Mistress Mena had told her about?

That he cared about her like she cared for him?

Their eyes met. He glanced at her lips, then back into her eyes.

She blushed and forced her eyes to stay on his, and not look at his own perfect lips right in front of her. She swallowed the frog in her throat that refused to allow her to speak.

Dev reached for her hand. Then he glanced behind her at the palace. His gaze cooled and he backed a half a step away from her.

Her shoulders sagged in disappointment. She wanted to see if the Guardian was watching them from his window. But the look on Dev's face answered the question for her without having to look for herself.

He turned and continued his stroll through the garden without saying anything else. She fell into step beside him. Her emotions were all over the place.

They walked in awkward silence for a few minutes, then Dev broke the silence with casual conversation. As if they hadn't just had an intimate moment together.

"Tell me about the rooms in the palace." His eyes wandered around the garden. They glanced up at the fourth floor from time to time. She pretended not to notice.

She didn't say anything at first.

"Indira," he said her name with such feeling.

Her heart skipped a beat.

"I'm sorry. About… everything. Please do not be angry with me. I do not want our meetings to be less enjoyable now because of my uncomfortable behavior." He sounded defeated.

Her eyes darted to his face. "Of course not, Dev."

She entertained his questions about the castle and tried to return to the light mood that normally existed between them. "What would you like me to tell you about?"

His shoulders relaxed and she tried not to be too disappointed. She told him about the paintings in the picture gallery. She went into as much detail as she could about several of them. The conversation was more awkward than normal.

"Perhaps you'd like to come see them?" she asked in a nervous voice and pointed at the door to the library.

Dev's body gave an involuntary shudder. "No, I would much prefer hearing you talk about them." He tried to sound normal, but his voice was stiff. "I can imagine them in my mind's eye from your wonderful descriptions."

Was Dev afraid of the Mountain Guardian? One moment he talked of destroying the Guardian, and the next he winced at the idea of facing him. Why should he be afraid if this was only a dream?

Or did he not want to spend more time with her?

Indira woke up more confused than she had been when she went to bed the night before. She groaned. Her neck and back were stiff from her curled up position in the library armchair.

"I should have gone back to bed." She stretched and twisted to work out the kinks.

To her surprise, her usual breakfast waited for her on the low table in front of her chair. Those little men had known she was there and brought it for her.

"Huh," she murmured to herself.

She ate a berry scone with honey butter and a small glass of fresh pressed orange juice. Then she headed to her new rooms on the fourth floor to ready herself for the day.

Eager to distract herself from her growing to-do list, she rushed up the stairs. She didn't want to think about her confusing encounter with Dev right now. Or her suffering people. Or ask herself the same questions over and over about what was real and why the Guardian refused to help her but allowed her to stay when he could force her to leave.

She tripped at the top of the stairs and landed flat on her face. "Oof!" she grunted.

A shuffling sound came from her left. She remained prone on the floor and turned her head ever so slightly so she could discover the source.

"Please let it be those little men," she whispered to herself.

It wasn't. The hooves and furry legs of the Guardian stood outside the door to his suite of rooms.

She groaned, again, and pushed herself off the floor. A gentleman would have rushed to her aid, but the Guardian stood frozen to the spot.

She smoothed her dress only to realize she still wore her too-thin nightgown. She hugged her arms around herself and glanced up at the Guardian with her sheepish eyes.

Would he make her leave now? Would he judge her because of her clumsiness? What would his reaction be?

"If you enjoy the library so much that you choose to sleep in it, you should spend more time there during the day. The palace does not need to be cleaned. No one lives here." The Guardian's words in someone else's voice might have sounded kind, thoughtful even. But from his strange mouth and in his gruff voice they sounded condescending.

She nodded and kept her mouth closed.

His eyes looked her up and down. He lowered his eyebrows as if in a frown, though his mouth could not frown, she supposed.

"You should get dressed," he stated flatly. A growl rumbled in his throat.

Her face burned.

"I'm sorry." She turned to enter her rooms.

She closed the door and leaned against it. She let out a long breath. She had tripped right in front of him. In her nightgown. After taking over the woman's suite without his permission and then not even spending the night in it!

And why was he upset that she spent her time cleaning and organizing? How else was she supposed to spend her time? If he didn't want her there, he could agree to help her and then she would leave!

She rushed into her room and shut the door a little harder than necessary. She flinched.

As she dressed herself, she thought about their exchange.

Maybe he was truly inviting her to spend time in the library, not judging her for sleeping in it? Perhaps he felt uncomfortable with her cleaning because she was not his servant, but a guest. Even if she was an uninvited one. And he had been right. It wasn't appropriate for her to stand and talk to him in his home while she wore her nightgown.

She should give him the benefit of the doubt. Just like she had told Dev when they met. Just because the Guardian looked like a beast on the outside didn't mean he was one on the inside.

Indira made her way downstairs. She knew she should probably do some cleaning. Even if the Guardian didn't think it was necessary. She loved the feeling of entering a room in disarray and turning it into something beautiful and functional again. Restoring it to the way it surely once was. It filled her heart to be able to see the change.

But, if she was honest with herself, she was tired from her not so restful night. And from sleeping in a chair. Her body was sore and stiff. And the Guardian had suggested she spend more time enjoying the library during the day. Perhaps she should take him up on his offer.

She perused all the different book collections. Volumes of historical texts with matching leather spines and shiny gold leaf. Oversized scientific treatises with hand drawn models on many of the pages. Shelves and shelves of epic poetry that Indira promised to return to. Books of music, theater scripts, tales of adventure and mystery. A series of books about the history of shipping caught her eye, as did a section of literary fiction about pirates.

The ladders, rolled to different sections, allowed Indira to view the library selections from floor to ceiling. There were so many. If she were to read every one, it would take several lifetimes!

The door to the library eased open. She felt like a spy as she looked down from halfway up one of the ladders, easily unnoticeable by whoever entered. Had the brownies come to deliver her lunch? She reached a foot down to descend but froze mid-step.

It was not a tiny man carrying a tray of food. It was the Mountain Guardian.

Sixteen

The Mountain Guardian loomed in the doorway of the library. His antlers turned side to side as he searched for Indira. His eyes stopped on the ladder, and he tipped his head back. In a blink, his eyes widened when he saw her so high above his head.

"Be careful!" he barked. She jumped from the suddenness of his words. Her foot slipped.

"Indira!" He cried and rushed toward the ladder.

She grabbed the rungs tight with her hands and repositioned her foot to steady herself. She smiled down at him. "I'm fine! Really!"

She nimbly climbed down the ladder.

He held out his strange, feathered hands to assist her, but did not touch her.

She planted her feet on the floor and turned to look up at him. He stood very close. His height and girth, and antlers, were intimidating. She shrunk a little.

He cleared his throat and took a long step back. "Apologies."

A smile lit up her own face. "No apologies necessary! I didn't fall. I'm all in one piece." She bent forward and pretended to inspect herself to make sure she was all there. "See?" She held out her arms and smiled at him again.

He nodded once. He stood there and stared.

Was he going to speak? Did he come here for a reason? Was she in trouble for being in the library? He had invited her to that morning! Her thoughts quickly spiraled.

"What book have you selected?" he blurted out.

The outburst startled her again, but because her feet were on the ground and she was not moving she didn't stumble or almost fall this time, thank goodness!

"Oh!" His question caught her off guard, too. "Um, I've been enjoying looking at all the different options. I haven't selected one yet."

"I see." His voice was deep and steady.

She couldn't tell if he spoke with a conceited air or if it was the nature of his kind to sound that way.

"I loved the one you gave me. You know, before," she tried to ease the tension.

His feathers ruffled a little around his neck.

"Do you have any more recommendations?" She encouraged him to say more.

He stared. He didn't move. He didn't say anything.

She waited. She wasn't in a hurry to be anywhere. She could wait as long as it took. The sooner he became friendly with her, the sooner he would agree to help her.

"Yes." He turned on his hooves and strolled with long strides across the library to the opposite wall. He slid his feathered finger along the spines of a collection she hadn't identified yet, then pulled a book from the shelf. It had gold leaf embedded in the embossed spine in a swirly design.

He returned to where she waited and reached forward to hand her the book.

She took it and he snapped his hand away from her before her fingers could accidentally touch his feathers.

She opened the book to identify it. "A mystery! Fun! Thank you!" She smiled up at him again.

His hooves shifted on the carpet. "You're welcome." He turned and walked out of the room without another word.

"Some progress is better than none," she said out loud after he had left. She stared at the closed door for several beats.

The natural light in the room dimmed. She moved toward the windows and tipped her head to look at the sky.

The always cloudless blue sky had filled with clouds. Thunder rumbled overhead. It looked as if it might rain. She sucked in a breath and waited.

The clouds did not open to release any water. In a few minutes, the storm had moved on and the sky was clear again.

She dropped her shoulders and settled herself on the sofa facing the garden to read the book the Guardian had recommended.

Indira read the last page of the book and closed the hard cover with a satisfying snap. She looked up and refocused her eyes. The book was fantastic! So much so that she hadn't gotten up once since she began reading it several hours earlier.

"It's evening!" The sun sank low behind the trees which turned the sky shades of pink, blue, and indigo.

She stood and stretched. "Oof, I feel stiffer than I did this morning! Maybe I *should* have cleaned today!" She rubbed her sore muscles and blinked her tired eyes.

Her stomach rumbled. "And I'm really hungry!" She looked around. No supper rested on any of the tables in the library.

Should she return to her room? Would the food be served there? There was a dining room on the opposite end of the palace from the library. She would also be satisfied eating in the kitchen.

A quick inspection of the kitchen provided nothing in the way of a meal. She knew a meal would have been prepared for her. The tiny men hadn't missed one yet. If the dining room proved to be a lost cause, she would return to the kitchen and pick through the pantry again.

She wandered past the bird room and the night-sky room, then turned to head toward the dining room. The smell of a warm stew and fresh baked bread met her nose. Her stomach grumbled again. She quickened her pace.

When she slid into the room, the majesty of the space rendered her speechless. The room was lit with tall candelabras set at even intervals along the length of a massive table big enough to seat dozens of people. The light shone all around the room and into the exposed beams and slanted roof above. Sconces placed within the squares of the wall trim work remained unlit, and the table candles cast long shadows away from the table and chairs. The corners of the room hid in shadow, but it did not give Indira an uneasy feeling, as she would have expected.

After she took it all in, she edged forward. The table was so long! It seemed silly for her to eat in here by herself.

"Welcome." A surprised, deep voice greeted her from the opposite end of the table from where she stood.

She jumped. She could just make out the shadows of the Mountain Guardian's antlers dancing on the far wall of the dining room.

She gulped. Maybe she should eat in her room.

"You may join me, if you wish," he declared in a stiff manner.

She stepped carefully around the end of the table and passed the two dozen chairs that lined the side she walked. She wanted to reach out and run her hands over their arched back, but kept her hands clasped tightly in front of her instead.

Dust did not cover the surfaces here, and that was not her doing. She hadn't spent any time here because the room was already clean.

The Guardian sat at the head of the table in a regal-looking velvet upholstered chair. Gilded paisley and floral designs trimmed the edges, arm rests, and legs.

The Guardian nodded at Indira. A setting of dishes filled with food rested at the chair to the Guardian's left. A place had been prepared for her.

She lowered herself into the chair and spread the cloth napkin over her lap. These were different dishes than the ones she had eaten from previously. They were meant for royalty. And the silverware was not plain but bore a crest design. Did it belong to the

Guardian? Did he have a people and a crest?

"Thank you," she whispered.

The Guardian looked uncomfortable to be eating with her. She attempted to make polite conversation, but he only gave short yes and no answers, even when the questions invited more.

Only a short while later, he finished his meal and placed his napkin on top of his plate.

"You plan to continue to stay?" He looked at her with a curious expression.

"Until you help my people." She tried to keep the impatience out of her voice. He knew this already. Why did he continue to ask?

He didn't respond. His chair scraped the wood floor, and he abruptly left the room.

"Well, that was fun," she murmured to herself. "Might as well enjoy the rest of my meal." She savored the rich flavors of the food and imagined her family eating alongside her at the enormous table.

Her brothers would grab handfuls of bread and potatoes and stuff their faces if they were here. Her sisters would be polite under their mother's watchful gaze, but when she wasn't looking, they would shove food into their mouths, too. Her father would regale them with stories from his latest journey…

Her heart sank. There was no latest journey anymore. There were no feasts to scarf down. No reason to scold the boys and glare at the girls for their terrible table manners, since there was barely enough food to go around. Everyone was subdued at mealtimes now.

Indira instantly lost her appetite, folded her own napkin, and placed it beside her plate on the table. She allowed her eyes to rove over all the food, wishing there was a way to send it to her family. But only the rain could save them now.

She half expected to dream about her family that night, for good or bad. She wanted to dream about Dev, of course, which knew to be foolish.

The last thing she wanted to see in her dreams was the hourglass.

She was sorely disappointed.

Seventeen

The hourglass continued to drain. It wouldn't be much longer before the top had emptied completely.

When she met Dev in the garden after running away from the hourglass in the dark, she was out of breath and clearly upset.

Dev wrapped his warm hands around her arms. "Look at me, Indi. What is it?"

She breathed hard. Sweat dotted her forehead and the back of her neck. Anxiety ate at her insides. She tried not to allow the panic to rise.

"The hourglass. My village. My family. Something

must be done. I fear their time is short. I don't know what to do!" Her words flew out of her mouth as fast as they entered her mind. They were a jumbled mess. She knew she sounded distraught but that's exactly how she felt.

Dev squeezed his eyes shut. He worked his jaw. A shadow fell across his face. "Indira. Instead of panicking, think about what you can control. How can you solve this problem?"

Indira stared with her mouth agape. "I can't! I can't make the rains come! I have no idea if they are safe or not. If they are in danger! There's nothing I can do!" Her volume was near a bellow by the time she finished.

"Breathe, Indi." Dev demonstrated for her.

She copied his breaths until her mind slowed and she could think clearly again. "Sorry, Dev. Yes, you're right."

Dev slid his hands down her arms. He took her hands. "You will be fine, Indira. I know you will. You could return to your home..."

"No," Indi insisted. Her stubbornness won over her anxiety. "Not until the Guardian helps me."

She turned her face toward the castle and roved her eyes over the windows to search for him. She knew he was probably there watching. Did he enjoy seeing her in a panic? She narrowed her eyes.

Dev rested a hand against her cheek and turned her face back toward him.

"If you refuse to leave, then is there something else you can do to ease your mind? A way to discover the welfare of your people?"

Indira paused to think. She ignored the heat and tingling where his hand touched her face and tried to focus on all of her *options. She had no way to send a message, as there was no staff or animals or anything at the palace.*

"Wait," she exclaimed. "There are animals!"

Dev looked confused.

"Sorry, talking to myself. It's a habit I have." She shrugged.

His eyes twinkled with delight.

"There is a roomful of birds! Perhaps I can have one of them carry a message home for me? I don't know how they would know where to go, though." She let go of Dev's hands and paced.

Could she draw them a map? No, that didn't make any sense. Birds couldn't read maps. Maybe one of them was, like, a homing pigeon or something? She could give it something from her home and it would know where to go? Was that even possible?

"It is. That's a perfect idea," Dev nodded.

"What?" Indi looked at him. Had she been speaking out loud? She thought it had been in her head.

She was so busy thinking about the birds and the possibility that Dev could read her mind that she didn't see a large stone in the path. Normally, in the waking world, it's something she would have tripped on, but she hadn't been clumsy in her dreams at all.

Dev shot his hand forward to catch her as if he fully expected her to trip.

When she didn't, he looked sheepish. "Sorry, I didn't want you to fall."

She gave him a warm smile.

He let out a relieved sigh. Because she was safe? Or for some other reason?

"So," Dev steered the conversation back to sending a message. "You'll use the birds?"

She pushed the other things out of her mind and focused back on the birds. "I'll have to locate some paper and pen so I can write a message. Then I'll need to figure out which bird would best be suited to the task. And think of something from home to give to the bird so it can find its way." She made a verbal list of the steps she would take in the morning.

"Perfect," Dev hooked her hand over his arm. "Shall we?"

He motioned for them to take their usual stroll through the garden. Then he paused. "Or would you like to accomplish your task at once?" He looked hopeful that she would choose to stay with him instead of leaving the garden and the dream.

Her lips pulled upwards. "I'll stay. The birds are asleep. None of them will want to fly at night. And I would have a much more difficult time finding the necessary supplies in the dark!"

It was a relief to spend the dream enjoying her time with Dev instead of fretting about everything else. She had a plan to find out if her family was safe. That's all she could do right now.

They settled beneath a weeping willow tree in full summer leaf. The breeze pushed the long branches in a soothing manner back and forth. Dev leaned against the tree trunk and Indira settled beside him. His nearness made her heart flutter.

When the pair was suitably relaxed, Indira stole a glance at Dev. She had to do something to calm the tension that definitely felt like good tension between them.

"If you could do anything right now, what would it be?" she asked him in a quiet voice.

He turned to look at her. She met his eyes.

"I... I would..." he stumbled over his words. His eyes flicked to her lips and his cheeks flushed.

His nervousness made her nervous, too. She pushed the thought away. This wasn't working the way she had hoped! She swallowed and attempted to switch tactics.

"How about this. If you could GO anywhere right now, where would you go?"

Dev leaned his head against the tree trunk and closed his eyes. "I would want to see your home. The way it was. You know, before." His soft voice held a lot of emotions, most of which Indira could not pinpoint.

"The way it will be again..." she whispered.

He slid his hand closer to hers. She didn't move away. Their hands nearly touched, but not quite.

"What will you do? If the Guardian does heal your lands?" His tone sounded sad.

Was he afraid that they would lose each other when she left the palace? It was something that she had chosen not to think about, but it was always there in the back of her mind. She wasn't ready for their departure from one another.

When she didn't answer right away, he prodded. "You mentioned before about sailing to sea?"

Her head nodded of its own accord. When her brain finally caught up with the conversation, she said, "Yes. Yes! I want to captain a ship. I know it sounds absurd, but I can't imagine staying in my village as someone's wife for the rest of my life. I want to see the world, to do great things."

Dev stayed quiet.

"What about you? What would you want to do? If you could leave…?" Was it an inconsiderate question?

He shook his head. "I do not know who I was before. How can I know who I will be after?" His words hung heavy between them.

Indira moved her hand to cover his. She squeezed. They sat in silence, holding one another's hands until Indira awoke.

Indira awoke feeling refreshed. Alive. Dev's face, his warm hand, filled her mind. Her stomach fluttered and she couldn't help the smile that spread across her face.

Then she remembered the beginning of her dream! She would send a message to her family today. Then she would know how dire the situation was. She would have answers. A sense of calm settled over her heart.

But what if the return message from her family contained dreadful news? What if her people were starving? Dying?

She squared her shoulders. If it was as bad as she feared, she would pressure the Guardian even harder to help. Maybe she would even throw a tantrum until he agreed. It worked for her younger siblings, even when they were well past the age of tantrums. She smirked at the idea.

She sat up in the large bed and dropped her feet over the side.

"What's this?" she spoke out loud even though, as usual, she was very much alone.

There on the nightstand stood a cage with a gorgeous red bird inside. Beside the cage rested a parchment, envelope, sealing wax and embossing stamp, an inkwell, and a feather pen.

Her eyes scanned the room. Where had these things come from? It was *exactly* what she needed in order to send a message. The only thing missing was something from her home.

There was no sense puzzling over the precious gift. She hurried to her bag to retrieve something. She found a dried bundle of forget-me-nots that grew in her land at the bottom of her bag. The color of the tiny blue flowers brought to mind Dev's dreamy eyes.

She shook her head and forced herself to focus on the task at hand. She penned a note to her parents, folded the paper, stuffed the envelope, and sealed it with wax. The symbol on the seal was the same design as the one on the flatware in the dining room. It must belong to the Guardian.

Her heart warmed.

Then it cooled. How had he known that she needed these things? He loomed over her and Dev in the dream garden. Was he somehow present, too? Did he eavesdrop on their conversations? The thought left goosebumps on her arms and neck.

"What does it matter, Indi? He knows what you want. Who cares if he's there while you dream?" She told herself the words out loud. But she wasn't convinced she believed them.

The little voice in the back of her mind told her to accept the gift for what it was. A kind gesture.

She sent the message with the bird. Now she had to wait to receive a reply. Then she would figure out what she was supposed to do next.

The library became her favorite place in the palace, but she continued to spend time making the other spaces feel like a home instead of an empty castle. When she left, whenever that was, after the Guardian helped her, she would leave him with the gift of a home he could fully enjoy. Who knew? Maybe he would even entertain guests in the future? She could imagine returning to attend an extravagant ball.

The thought seemed absurd, but she told herself that it was not an impossible idea.

After several days of reading intermingled with cleaning, she had not received a response from home.

And she continued to dream each night of the hourglass running low on sand.

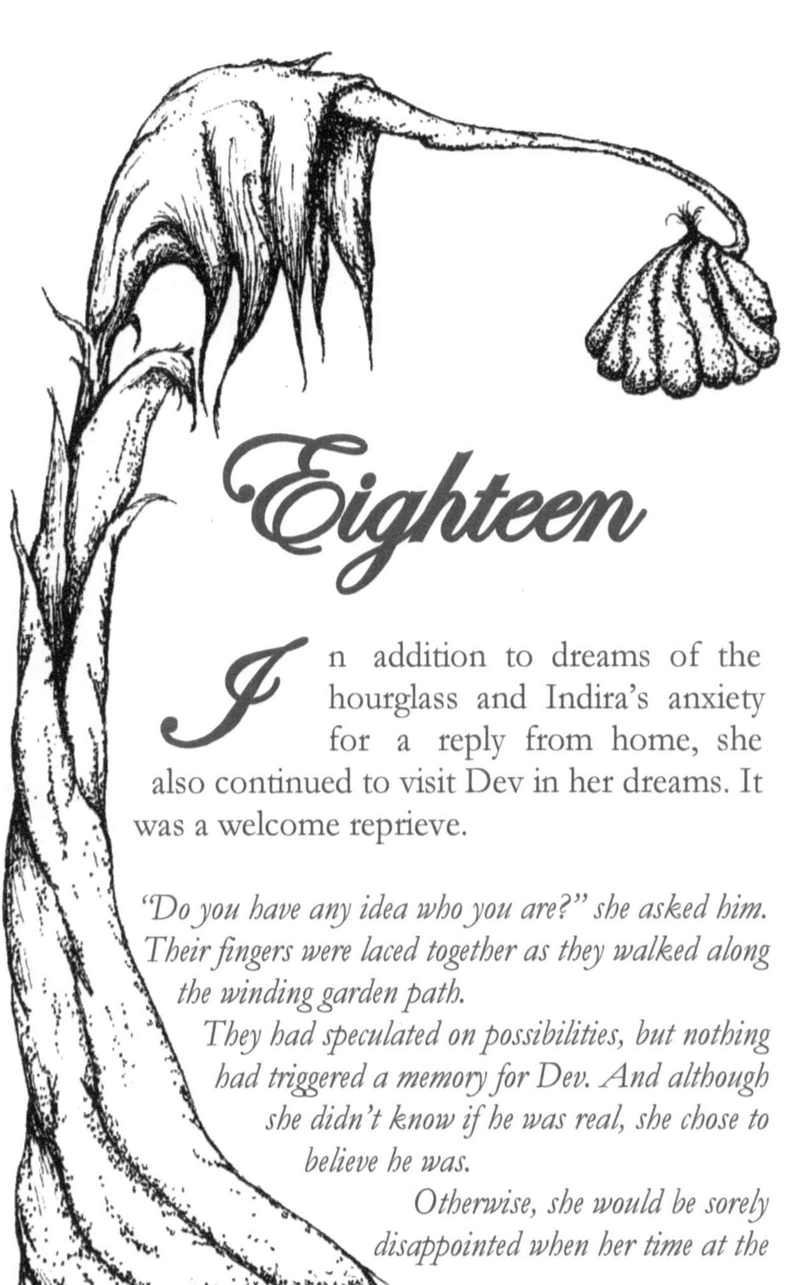

Eighteen

In addition to dreams of the hourglass and Indira's anxiety for a reply from home, she also continued to visit Dev in her dreams. It was a welcome reprieve.

"Do you have any idea who you are?" she asked him. Their fingers were laced together as they walked along the winding garden path.

They had speculated on possibilities, but nothing had triggered a memory for Dev. And although she didn't know if he was real, she chose to believe he was.

Otherwise, she would be sorely disappointed when her time at the palace came to an end. She was determined that once she left, she would discover who he really was and find him.

Dev's mood this night was light. She had a feeling he was covering up deeper emotions in order to keep her preoccupied from her own troubles.

In a mock serious tone, he answered her question. "Probably a pirate." He stole a glance at her.

She pinched his arm. "You are not a pirate!" she laughed.

"Oh, really? How do you know?" He answered with pretend hurt pride.

"Dev! Seriously! You're not a pirate!"

"Give me three good reasons why you believe I am not a pirate."

Indira pinched her lips to think.

"And could you please make an adorable scrunched up face while you do?" he teased.

Her heart fluttered.

"Not a pirate reasons?" he prodded.

"Right. One- you are built totally wrong to be a pirate." Indira stepped away from him but did not let go of his hand. She pretended to appraise his stature with a studious eye. "No, indeed."

"What?" Dev stilled. "You're saying my sturdy physique would not do well on a pirate ship?" He acted affronted.

She laughed. He couldn't hold his laughter any longer.

They both knew that his shorter than average height and leaner than average muscle tone did not scream "pirate" as an occupation.

"Two?" He feigned disdain.

"Two. You have totally the wrong complexion for a pirate. Your skin would burn in the sun faster than you could imagine."

He rolled his eyes at the obvious truth to her statements.

"Three." She taunted him with her third point. "You are far too kind to be a pirate." She shot him a silly grin.

His face flickered between happiness and despair for a second. He regained his composure. "You know nothing about me! How do you know I am too kind to be a pirate? Perhaps I would commandeer your ship and take Captain Indira and throw her into the brig!" He poked her side in a tickle.

She shrieked and wiggled away from him. "No way," she announced. "Captain Indi would never allow it!"

She mimed unsheathing a sword. "Arm yourself, you scallywag!"

"I'll make you walk the plank!" Dev shouted as he chased her through the garden.

When Indira awoke in the morning, she beamed from ear to ear.

That day's cleaning took Indira to the second picture room on the second floor of the palace. She hadn't gone back since that first day when she had merely peeked in.

She set down her bucket, scrub brush, and dust rags and stared at the walls.

They were not decorated with painting of animals and landscapes. They were people. All of them!

Her eyes roved from one painting to the next.

Dozens and dozens of eyes stared back at her. A chill ran down her spine.

"It's not creepy, Indi. They're just paintings."

But so many strange things had already happened here, that she wasn't totally convinced.

"Dusting, floors. That's all this room needs. I'll be out of here in no time."

She forced herself to focus on her tasks instead of all the eyes. But when it came time to dust, she couldn't help herself.

She read the name engraved on a plaque on the bottom of each picture. Then she looked into their eyes. She thought of what their lives might have been like. When had they lived? Was this their home? Had the Guardian taken it from them? Is that where the rumors of his ruthlessness came from?

It didn't match the character of the creature she had spent time with, though. Even though that time was limited. He was not a monster. She didn't think he would conquer anyone or take things that didn't belong to him.

But she *had* spent very little time with him. He could have a dark past that she knew nothing about.

The eyes in one of the paintings seemed familiar to her. She stared at them for a long time. The woman had strawberry blond, curly hair that fell over her shoulders. Freckles dotted her petite nose. Her red lips had a quirk to them, like she knew something Indi didn't.

"With all the other magical things about this place, the least you could do is tell me!" she whispered to the woman as she dusted the picture frame. It was the last one.

She stood with her hands on her hips and scanned the room again. It felt more like a home with a close-knit family than a creepy gallery now.

"Goodbye!" she called over her shoulder at the paintings as she closed the door.

At dinner that night, Indi asked the Guardian about the paintings.

"Who are all those people on the second floor?" she asked between bites of her roasted sweet potatoes.

The Mountain Guardian froze with his fork halfway to his beak-nose. "Excuse me?" he asked in confusion.

Indi laughed. That had sounded weird! "The paintings in the gallery on the second floor, not real people!" She met his eyes.

He looked down at his plate. He returned his fork to his food, scooped a larger bite of his own sweet potatoes, and stuffed them into his mouth.

He chewed slowly and avoided eye contact with her.

Was he employing the same tactic with her that she frequently used on her mother? A full mouth can't answer questions. She smiled to herself, but then remembered the question about the paintings. And where the people had come from.

"Are they people you know?" She asked again. This

time with less humor in her voice.

"No," he stated.

She sighed. "Then who are they? Why do you have a whole gallery of paintings of people you don't know?"

He didn't reply.

"Fine, don't tell me." She set her fork on her plate. She had lost her appetite. "I'm worried about my village. Guardian, will you please help me save them?" Her voice had gone from annoyed to pleading in two sentences.

He dropped his eyes to the table. Was he not going to answer her?

Her anger flared.

She stood suddenly. "I won't leave until you agree to do this. I can outlast your refusals. I will continue to ask you every single day until you agree!" Her voice rose. She didn't quite yell, but she came pretty close.

So much for kindness. She scolded herself but pushed the thought away. She didn't even care about that anymore!

His eyes met hers. They were troubled. Ice formed beneath his hands on the arms of his chair. His breath fogged when he spoke in such a quiet voice that she almost couldn't hear.

"I can't. I'm sorry." He stood and icy footprints followed him out of the room.

Thunder cracked in the sky and lightning flashed bright through the windows. Icy pebbles tapped against the other side of the glass.

Only a moment later, the weather stilled again. The sky cleared.

Indi sank back into her chair. She rubbed her forehead. She had angered the Guardian. Had all of her efforts to appeal to his gentler side been wasted by her childish behavior? Had she ruined her chance of him agreeing to help her?

"You're such a fool, Indi. Now you'll need to undo what you've done. Hopefully he will accept your apology."

Even though he hadn't agreed to help save her people, he did treat her very well. Kindness would have been a better way to convince him to help her than a childlike tantrum.

Indira hurried back to her room to write a sincere apology letter for the Guardian. Along with her words of gratitude for his kindness, and her deepest apologies for her inappropriate behavior, she extended him an invitation to join her the following day for a picnic in the garden.

Indira didn't mention her embarrassing behavior to Dev in her dream that night. She couldn't bring herself to point out her flaws to this man that she had grown to care for. What would he think of her if he knew?

She kept the conversation on more superficial things. She talked about the latest book she had selected from the library. She told him about one of the voyages she took on her father's ship.

He soaked in all of her words but didn't speak much himself. Could he somehow know about her outburst with the Mountain Guardian? The thought made her feel disgusted with herself.

Not only was he quiet, but Dev also had a hint of sorrow in his eyes when he looked at her.

She couldn't exactly ask him what was on his mind while she willingly kept her own troubles to herself.

Their visit together didn't last long. The sky was a little less bright than usual, as if it reflected both of their moods. And the Guardian did not spy on them from his window on the fourth floor.

Everything was out of sorts.

It didn't surprise her when she didn't dream about the hourglass.

The following morning, Indi found a picnic basket in the back of the pantry. She filled it to overflowing with everything edible she could find. Cheeses, nuts, breads, crackers, spreads, butters. She included fruits and vegetables that she picked from the garden and arranged it all in a pleasing display inside the basket. She folded up one of the cloths that had covered furniture in the sitting room to use as a picnic blanket, and made sure she had napkins for cleanliness, and tin cups to drink water from.

Her message had asked the Guardian to meet her in the library for the picnic at the usual lunch hour. They would leave through the library doors and head into the garden to share their meal. She would show him that she could be grateful and wasn't a spoiled girl who stomped her feet and cried when she didn't get her way.

She waited for nearly half an hour for the Guardian to join her. Her stomach rumbled. She waited longer.

"He can join me in the garden if he decides to come." Disappointment weighed her words and her heart.

She pushed open the door and wandered to her favorite spot in the garden beside the creek. She spread out the blanket and settled herself on top of it. She unpacked the food and arranged it in preparation for a shared meal. Then she folded her hands in her lap to wait.

She popped a cherry tomato into her mouth. The sweet juice ran down her throat. She balanced the sweetness of it with a chunk of the sharp cheese.

That made her thirsty, so she poured some water into her cup.

She glanced at the library. No sign of the Guardian.

She closed her eyes and enjoyed the warm sunshine. She forced herself to relax and not worry about, well, about everything. She focused on the garden. The sweet smell of the flowers. The buzzing of the bees.

She had brought some honey from the pantry. She opened her eyes and drizzled some honey on a cracker. The smoothness and sweetness nudged her eyes shut again. It was delicious.

She looked at the library again. Then her eyes found the window on the fourth floor. The Guardian was there. He watched her with a hand on the curtain. She stared back at him.

She couldn't see his eyes against the dark feathers of his face through the reflective surface of the window.

What was he thinking while he watched her sneak bites of the picnic she had prepared for them to share? Was he angry with her? Would he come down to sit with her?

Nineteen

Indira sighed and lowered her gaze. When she glanced up again, he was no longer there.

She held her breath and waited for him to join her. But instead of his presence the only things she gained were heavy raindrops from the suddenly cloudy sky. She was soaked in minutes. She threw everything into the basket and ran back to the library. Her tears mingled with the rain running down her face.

"I haven't heard anything from home. I have no idea if my people are safe. What if they aren't? What if they think I abandoned them, and they have shunned me? What if they left and I'll never be able to find them?"

Indira's imagination ran away with her while she poured her heart out to Dev in her dream.

"And why won't the Guardian help me?" she continued. "He says he can't. But he clearly can control the weather. He's done it a number of times lately when he's upset with me." She sighed and groaned. She rubbed her forehead. "Am I wasting my time here? What am I even doing anymore?"

Dev rubbed her back. He sat beside her on the stone bench in the garden, much closer than the first time they had spoken there together. His rhythmic touch calmed her enough that it slowed the words from tumbling out of her mouth.

She looked at Dev. "Thank you."

He gave her a tender look. She blushed beneath his gaze.

"What would you do, if this was your situation to maneuver?" She asked for his advice in a quiet voice.

He paused to think before he answered. "I would want to be with my family." His voice broke. He had a longing look in his eyes. He broke eye contact and looked at the ground.

Did he have a family? Was he real? She still didn't know. But one thing she did know.

"I must stick it out. I cannot give up if I even have the slightest chance of helping my people."

Dev didn't respond. He supported her with his presence.

How was she going to convince the Guardian to help her? To forgive her for her unpleasant behavior? To think of her as a friend instead of a thorn in his side?

She caught sight of the rose pendant in her

reflection in the glass as she gazed out her own window onto the garden below. She wrapped her fingers around it. Mistress Mena had given it to her and told her that it would offer her protection from danger.

Indira knew that red roses symbolized passion and love. She blushed when her mind instantly thought of Dev.

But yellow roses signified joy, transformation, and new beginnings.

She didn't know what color the rose on the pendant was meant to represent. Could it be both? Was the transformation for her people and land? Or was it something that she needed to change about herself?

How was she to find joy if the Guardian wouldn't help her? And how could she love a man she didn't even think was real?

Indira could almost hear the old woman's advice as if she was with her now. *"The Mountain Guardian is dangerous. He views himself superior to mere mortals. He has a violent temperament that demands respect."*

But Indira had not known him to be violent at all. If anything, he was passive.

"He is a beast with no love in his heart, even for someone as sweet as you."

Could that be true? Was there no hope of convincing him to help her at all?

No. She didn't believe that. She would do it. She would prove her worth to the Guardian and *make* him want to help her. Her mind swirled through all of the possibilities.

What was one thing about the Guardian that most people probably misunderstood? Something she could prove that she didn't agree with to show him that she deserved his help.

That he was a monster. A beast. She knew he was not. She would show him.

The most un-monster-like thing she could think of was a banquet. She had never been to one herself, but she had read about them in books, both fiction and non-fiction. She could totally pull this off.

And she would ask the brownies that always snuck around the place for their help.

While the little men worked on a menu, Indira created a formal invitation. She wrote in swirly letters that a banquet was to be held in two days' time and that the Guardian's presence was requested.

He hadn't accepted the invitation to the picnic. But he would come to this, right? It was just dinner after all. She hoped he would.

A note for her helpers left instructions to come up with a meal that would be fit for a king, but they needn't provide enormous quantities of food since it was only the two of them who would be dining. Although, the Guardian was rather large. The men would know how much to provide.

Indira entered the closet filled with clothes that

were exactly her size. She had enjoyed wearing some of them but had stuck with the simpler fabrics and designs. She did not require anything luxurious for cleaning the palace and reading in the library or garden.

But for the banquet she wanted to feel special. It was not to be a romantic evening, but she wanted to prove to the Guardian that she was worthy of his assistance. That she respected him and would be eternally grateful if he helped her. In her mind, this was her last chance to impress him.

She perused all of her clothing options. She stopped and froze when she saw the dress in front of her.

"It's perfect," she whispered to herself.

The banquet wasn't until the following day. She would wait until then to try it on, although she could tell by looking that it would fit her just right.

She knew the Guardian watched her and Dev in the garden. And she wasn't sure if he could hear their conversation. She said nothing about the banquet. She didn't want to give any hints of what she had planned away.

Dev kept glancing at her. He seemed nervous, like he knew she was hiding something this time.

She kept the conversation light and enjoyed his company. A small part of her wondered what would happen after the following evening.

If the Guardian agreed to help her, she would leave. Would she continue to dream of Dev after she returned home? Or was he part of the magic of the castle? She didn't want to think about never seeing him again, even if it was just in her dreams.

But she also wondered what would happen if the Guardian continued to refuse. How long could she stay here? What else could she do to convince the Guardian to help?

Unwanted and uninvited, the hourglass loomed in the back of Indira's mind as she awoke from her slumber.

The day of the banquet dragged on. Her nerves left her with no appetite during the day. She skipped all the food offerings from the pair of miniature men.

She had to find something to distract herself or she would make herself sick and have to skip the banquet herself!

She visited all the whimsical rooms in the castle. If this was to be her last day here, she wanted to see it all one last time.

The birds treated her to a long performance of songs. She basked in the moist air and beautiful music until they were finished.

She spent time lying on the soft floor of the night sky room, staring at the stars, and imagining she could see far past them into the blackness. There were so many!

She studied the paintings of animals and landscapes. She hadn't ever asked the Mountain Guardian where those ones had come from. He probably wouldn't have told her if she had, though.

She even braved the picture gallery full of portraits.

She stopped in front of the woman holding a secret again. Something about this one drew her in. Those eyes. They reminded her of someone.

No one back home had blue eyes. The only person she knew with eyes that color was Dev.

She squinted and leaned closer. She studied the eyes in the painting. They were the exact same pale forget-me-not blue of Dev's eyes. Her heart fluttered every time she thought of him. She hoped she wouldn't lose him forever when she left this place, whenever that would be.

As evening drew near, Indira returned to her rooms. She retrieved the stunning dress and prepared herself for the most important meal of her life. The entire future of her people rested on her shoulders. The weight was tremendous. She refused to let them down.

Indira removed her plain daytime clothing. She slipped the silky, sleeveless underlayer of the dress over her head and allowed it to drop over her petite frame. The fabric was soft against her skin. The hem reached her ankles. It was the perfect length.

She ran her hands over the goldenrod-colored lightweight fabric of the dress. She took a deep breath and took it off the hanger.

She pulled the dress over her head the same way she had the underlayer. The bodice had tiny clasps on the side seam. She nimbly clasped each of them together. She ran her hands down the skirt from her waist to her thighs to smooth the fabric.

The honey-colored garnet-like gomed gemstone encrusted bodice hugged her chest tight enough to flatter her figure but comfortable enough that she could breathe easily. More of the same gemstones dangled from the edges of the cap sleeves that just covered her shoulders but left her arms bare.

Beneath the bodice, the skirt flared into a cone that circled her feet, though the hem didn't quite touch the floor. The skirt swung in a satisfying swish when she turned side to side, but it was not so full that it would be awkward to sit down for the entirety of a several course banquet. A wide border of the gomed beads had been stitched into a wide border around the bottom of the skirt in a delicate pattern that imitated lace.

Beside the dress in the closet, another hanger held a large, sheer rectangle of jewel-adorned fabric a shade lighter than the golden color of the dress. A fringe of gomed beads clinked when she removed it from the hanger. She draped the fabric over her elbows and around her back. The long ends hung to the exact length of the hem of her dress.

Indira couldn't help but smile wide. The dress, the fabric, the jewels. It was all so beautiful.

She skipped to the dressing table at the back of the closet. Opulent jewelry rested on velvet drawer linings. She selected a wide gold choker necklace that hugged her neck and dipped to match the rounded neckline of the dress.

She chose a narrow necklace with a honey garnet pendant on it. Instead of wearing it around her neck, she attached it with hairpins down the center part of her dark hair. The pendant rested in the middle of her forehead.

A half dozen thin gold bracelets jingled with her movements on one of her wrists. She wore a bejeweled bracelet as an anklet. A pair of soft matching golden slippers finished the ensemble.

Indira stood back to inspect herself in the full-length mirror. She twisted and turned to make sure everything was in the right place. When she was satisfied, she gazed at her reflection with the eyes of an outsider.

She looked like a princess!

Tears stung her eyes. She had never been considered exceptionally beautiful before. Her people didn't generally adorn themselves in such luxurious fabrics and trinkets. But at that moment she felt pretty for the first time.

She swiped her eyes and couldn't suppress her smile. She squealed. Then she forced herself to calm down and commit everything to memory so she could tell her sisters all about it.

The grandfather clock in the hall struck the hour. The chimes still sounded to her like they called her name. It was time for the banquet.

Twenty

Sconces around the perimeter of the dining hall held two bright candles each. The rich woods and opulent rugs glowed warmly in the candlelight. Tall white tapered candles stood in a row on a table behind where the Mountain Guardian usually sat.

The curtains were pulled back to allow the glow of the evening light to shine in through the wall of windows.

Candelabras sat at regular intervals down the center of the table. Berry garlands adorned with small gold tealight candles wove between the tall candelabras.

Enormous fresh golden sunflowers had been laid among the garlands here and there.

Sugar had been expertly shaped into stunning formations and placed amidst the garland. How had the little men done it?

The room was bright with light from all angles.

Dark red and gold fabrics draped over the table and hung over the sides. Indira's and the Guardian's places had been set with gilded plates, golden flatware, and crimson napkins tucked inside golden napkin rings.

Indira had requested a banquet fit for a king. Her helpers had fulfilled her wishes. More than she could have ever imagined!

Trays of food filled the entire width of the table at the far end where Indira and the Guardian would sit for the feast.

Wood-smoked salmon lay on a bed of greens atop a golden platter. Lemon slices sat in a tidy row along the length of the fish. Dill and garlic decorated the top.

Two beef and bacon pies sat on a rectangular platter side by side. The crust was shiny and perfectly golden.

Pink crayfish had been arranged in a circle around a clear glass goblet filled with a savory dipping sauce.

Candied fruits glistened in the candlelight. Pomegranates, cut in half to expose the jewel seeds on the inside, tempted Indi atop a glass pedestal bowl.

Spiced poached pears so dark purple they were near brown in a warm cider sauce sent a sweet and spicy aroma to her nose.

Miniature berry tarts bled purple juice from underneath cheese melted over the tops.

There were dishes of purple cabbage, vibrant artichokes, perfectly steamed asparagus, roasted golden potatoes, tender beef thinly sliced, and honey glazed duck served with rich gravy.

To cleanse the palate between courses the men had provided jellies and wafers alongside exotic fruits, nuts, and flavored butter.

Warm cider steamed from inside the pair of gilded goblets at both place settings.

Indira slowly lowered herself into her chair. Her eyes couldn't stop taking it all in. Her senses were overwhelmed by the sights and smells. In a good way!

Tears stung her eyes again. She swallowed and forced them to stay put.

She folded her hands in her lap. Her fingers danced with her nerves. Her palms sweated.

She kept glancing at the door. Would the Guardian come? Would she end up partaking of this magnificent feast alone? She didn't think she'd be able to.

Just when she thought he would never appear, the Guardian's large frame filled the dining room doorway.

She breathed a sigh of relief. She straightened her posture and gave him a warm smile.

"Surprise!" she announced in a friendly voice.

The Guardian moved slowly down the length of the opposite side of the table. His eyes roved over everything. His face was impossible to read.

What was he thinking? Was he pleased? Was he

angry?

When he arrived at his place at the head of the table, he stood with his feathered hands on the back of his throne-like chair. He perused all the food offerings in a blink, then his eyes landed on Indira.

She held her breath and braced herself for his reaction.

He pulled the chair away from the table and lowered himself into his seat.

"I'm glad you came." She removed her napkin from the napkin ring and spread it out over her lap. "Do you like it?" She gestured at the stunning display of food.

The Guardian didn't look at the food. He kept his eyes on her. "Yes." The candlelight reflected in his dark pupils. His eyes shone.

Indira reached for one of the platters to help herself to the food.

"Allow me," he offered and reached for her plate.

"Thank you!" She passed her plate to him, careful not to touch his feathered hands.

He looked at her with a question as he pointed at each food offering. She either nodded or shook her head to indicate what she would like. When he had given her a little bit of all the things she wanted, he returned her plate.

"It all looks and smells so good!" She studied her plate with excitement. What would she eat first?

The Guardian sat still in his chair.

"Aren't you going to eat, too?" she quizzed him.

He jumped the slightest bit when her eyes met his. Then he quickly looked away. "Oh. Yes." He served himself his supper.

When he had filled his own plate, Indira picked up her fork. "I can't wait to try, well, everything!"

Fortunately, her appetite had returned the instant the Guardian had arrived. Her nerves were a little tighter than usual, but she was starving after not eating for the entire day!

She made small talk with the Guardian as she ate. As usual his responses were short and curt.

Her heart sank a little. She wanted him to be in a good mood when she asked him about helping. Again.

She ate slowly and savored every bite. She sat back in her seat and rested her napkin on the table. "That was… amazing! Your helpers sure know how to prepare a decent meal."

The Guardian grumbled something under his breath. She thought she heard the word "pest" but couldn't be sure.

So, don't talk about the little men. Got it.

She opened her mouth to ask him if he would help her and her people.

He started to speak at the same time.

She let out a nervous laugh.

His face remained expressionless.

She gulped. "Go ahead, you first."

He cleared his throat and gripped the arms of his chair tight. "Thank you for planning this… surprise."

He growled the last word. "I am grateful for your thoughtfulness." His words were stiff and formal.

She hadn't managed to soften him up at all. Her heart sank. "You are welcome." She paused. She debated whether to say what she was thinking or not. Should she keep things formal between them? She wished for him to view her as a friend, not a nuisance.

She let out a sigh and dropped her shoulders. She placed her hands flat on the table and leaned toward him a little. "Guardian, thank you for your kindness in allowing me to stay in your home and disrupt your routines. I understand why you live alone." She swallowed and forced herself to continue. "I know people see you as a monster."

He stiffened. His eyes widened and leaned away from her. She had offended him.

She hurried to continue. "But I see that you are not a monster. I do think you are lonely. I think you would do well to allow more people into your life. It could bring you so much joy."

She held her breath.

He didn't take his eyes off her face. He didn't blink. She could barely tell if he breathed.

"Indira, I…" he started to say, then he clamped his mouth shut.

"Yes?" She encouraged him to speak.

"It's nothing." He dropped his gaze and remained still. Frost built up beneath his fingers on the arms of his chair.

"Will you allow me to be your friend?" she asked in a timid voice.

He didn't answer.

"Will you help me and my people? Please?" She whispered the last word. Her throat tightened. She couldn't speak anymore.

He sat still as a statue.

She waited. She would wait as long as it took. She was desperate.

"Please, I'll do anything…" she started to beg.

"I cannot." His voice was low but firm.

Her heart cracked. Heat rose up her neck. "Why? Why won't you help me?" she choked on her tears. "I know you are not unfeeling. We would be forever grateful. *I* would be forever grateful." Tears dripped down her cheeks.

His own eyes glistened. Lightning flashed outside. Thunder boomed so close that the windows rattled.

"That! That's what I need you to do! Send the rain to my home. Please!" She swung her arm toward the window. She knocked over her goblet of warm cider. It spilled across the table and soaked into the tablecloth.

He looked down at his plate. His voice was flat again. "You should leave. Take your people somewhere safe. There is nothing I can do for you."

The tablecloth continued to soak up the puddle of cider. Indira stared at the Guardian in disbelief.

"That's your answer?" she whispered. "I came here

because I believed you could help me. I can see now that it was a mistake." She pushed her chair back from the table, stood, and turned away to leave the room.

"I should have helped you sooner." His voice reached her ears, the volume barely above a whisper.

Indira froze. She waited for him to say more. She didn't look back at him but kept her eyes on the floor at her feet.

"I didn't think you would actually stay." He continued in a pained voice. "That was my mistake for which I am truly sorry. But it is too late now."

Indira took a deep breath, then let it out slowly. If she turned to face him, would he stop talking? Did he have more to say? She waited.

"You have done so much for the palace. For me." He let out a sorrowful moan. "Goodbye, Indi."

She heard his chair slide on the floor. His heavy footsteps hurried away from her.

She turned on her heels. He was gone. A hidden doorway in the wall at the back of the dining hall stood ajar.

She stared. His absence loomed larger than his foreboding presence.

Her mind raced. What had happened? And why did he call her Indi? She had never told him that she went by that name. How did he know?

Before she could follow in his footsteps to discover more, one of the tiny men rushed into the room. He didn't speak but held a water-logged envelope in his hands. He extended it toward her.

She looked back and forth between the man and the open door. She took the envelope from the little man. He scurried out of the main entrance to the dining hall.

She recognized the writing on the outside of the envelope. She tore it open and unfolded the sopping paper inside. She skimmed the words, and her hand flew to her mouth.

Twenty-one

The storm continued to rage outside the palace. Indira paced around her suite in the castle, back in the nightgown she had claimed from the closet. Should she go to the Guardian? Should she return home to help her people?

She felt as if her heart was the hourglass and all of her hopes for the future slipped away with every beat.

She threw herself on the bed and screamed into her pillow.

The evening had been so peaceful. The food amazing. Her dress the most gorgeous thing she had ever worn.

And now it was all over. And her people were in trouble.

Logically she knew she couldn't travel in this storm. She had no mount. She had no idea which way was home. She was stuck.

She lay on her back and stared at the ceiling. She would leave the Guardian alone for tonight, and then in the morning she would ask for his assistance in returning home. He had told her she should. He would at least help her get there. Right?

"I hope so," she whispered.

Eventually sleep came, though she wasn't sure if it would ever arrive.

Ice coated the entire outside of the palace. Frost covered every blade of grass, stem, leaf, and blossom in the garden. The babbling brook stood still. Frozen.

She sucked in a breath. The cold stabbed her throat and lungs.

"Dev! Where are you?" she yelled and turned in a frantic circle.

"I'm here." His voice came from behind her.

She whipped around.

He looked distraught. Fearful.

"I'm so sorry, Dev. This is all my fault. I upset the Guardian. My people are in real danger from famine and thirst." She twisted her hands together and blinked away the tears from her eyes.

Dev rushed toward her and took both her hands in his. "No, Indi. This is not your fault. It is mine."

She lowered her eyebrows and frowned. "I don't understand."

She wasn't even sure he was real. How could this be his fault?

He dropped her hands and ran his through his red hair. He paced back and forth in front of her. "I should have told you sooner," he murmured to himself.

"What do you mean? Tell me what?" Indira kept her eyes on his frantic movements.

Her heart beat against her ribcage. The Guardian had let her down so completely. Was Dev about to do the same? Why was her mind playing tricks on her like this? Was she supposed to break?

Her distress must have been written all over her face.

Dev hurried back to her and wrapped his arms around her in a desperate embrace.

She gasped with surprise. And also, from the way her heart leapt in her chest from the intimate contact. She held him tight with her arms around his waist.

He took deep breaths into her hair as if to control his own emotions. "I am so sorry, Indi."

When he released her, she took a step back. Her regular daytime clothes that always appeared on her body in the dreams had transformed to the princess quality clothing from the banquet.

"You are so beautiful," he brushed a strand of hair from the side of her face. "Dance with me?"

Music came from the now open doors of the library still shrouded in ice.

She had no idea what was going on. She was thoroughly confused. But the admiration in his eyes glued her to the spot.

He placed one hand on her waist and held her other hand

with his. His touch made her skin tingle. She no longer felt the cold from the wintry garden.

He pulled her close and spread his palm flat against her back. She wrapped her hand underneath his arm and up over his shoulder. She closed her eyes and breathed in his familiar scent.

How was his scent familiar? She had never been this close to him before.

Little pieces started to come together in her mind.

Dev knew she was clumsy, even though she wasn't in the dreams. The Guardian knew what she and Dev talked about in the dreams, even though he stood sentinel on the fourth floor behind a pane of glass. The Guardian had called her Indi...

She gasped and took a step back to peer into Dev's eyes.

He gave her a knowing look. Grief pinched the corners of his eyes.

"Dev, are you... is he...?" She looked up at the window. The Guardian was not there tonight.

"I am sorry. I should have told you sooner." Dev choked on his words.

She didn't know what to think. Dev was the Guardian? How was that even possible? It didn't make any sense.

"I'm so confused!" She rubbed her forehead.

Dev kept his distance. The absence of his touch made her feel cold. Colder than the ice that surrounded them.

"Tell me. Please?" she whispered while she locked her eyes onto his.

His shoulders sank. "I am the Guardian."

Dev heaved a deep sigh and turned his face away from her. Her heart cracked from the distance between them. Not just physically, but from the truth she was about to hear.

"You have said you know of the legend regarding the Mountain Guardian?" Dev avoided eye contact. He twisted his hands in the nervous manner he had done when she first met him.

He didn't wait for her to answer. "I do not know where I came from or who I was before… this." He pointed at the castle. "All I know is my name."

"Dev," Indira whispered.

His eyes darted to meet hers, then he turned away from her again.

"The last thing I remember is wandering through a blizzard on a snowy mountain. This snowy mountain. I was freezing. Sure I was going to die. Then the next thing I knew I was inside the castle. But I had become a monster." Dev's voice was bitter and hateful.

The disgust he felt for the Mountain Guardian was directed at himself.

"No, Dev…" Indira started to say.

He cut her off. "You saw what I have become. In the waking world, at least. Cursed to be a half man half monster. Doomed to be alone forever, with no memory of a past. A family. A life."

Dev doubled over and groaned. He clutched his stomach. "It is too much to bear alone. But I was fearful of what I might do if I encountered another person. So, I spread the rumors of the prisoners to keep people away. I do not know why I have been cursed to live this way. But you deserve so much more."

He straightened with a pained look on his face. He met her eyes. "I am a monster, Indira. Until you came along, I did not know what my human form looked like. When you arrived, I found myself here, in the garden, with you. It brought me hope that perhaps there is still a man inside the beast. But I do not know how to release him. Me." His voice cracked, and he turned fully away from her.

Indira didn't know what to say. How to comfort him. Her heart skipped a beat. He was real. She had not fallen in love with a figment of her imagination.

Her mouth opened as she was about to tell him she loved him, regardless of his unfortunate circumstances. But the words that came out were not the ones she intended to say.

"Why wouldn't you help me? From the beginning?" she asked in a soft voice.

"I am a monster, Indi." His words were muffled as he folded in on himself. "If I was to come to your home and bring the rain, I would be run out of your village. Possibly even hunted, imprisoned, or worse." He shook his head.

"But you're not a monster," she insisted.

He turned around. Anger danced in his eyes. "You saw what I am! There is no other word for it." His voice was hard as stone.

"But I will be with you." She took a half step closer to him. "I will keep you safe. We can go, right now!" Hope blossomed in her chest. They would heal her land. Then together they would find a cure for his curse.

He shook his head. "I am afraid it is too late now."

"You said that before. How is it too late? I don't understand, Dev. Please tell me!" Her words were desperate.

He looked away. Fidgeted. Then met her eyes. "As my feelings for you have grown, my control over the elements has *diminished." He searched her eyes with hope and fear in his.*

She studied his face. "You're feelings for me?" What was he saying?

He swallowed hard. His voice came out raspy. "I love you, Indi. You are pure of heart. You are kind. You didn't judge me when you saw me. Me as I truly am." He gestured to the icy palace.

She stepped closer. She placed a hand on his chest. "This is who you truly are," she whispered.

He gripped her hand against his chest with his own. He rested his other hand on the side of her face. He searched her eyes.

"As long as my love for you remains, as long as you remain in my life, I will not be able to bring the rain to your lands. In order for me to save you and your people, I must let you go. Forever."

He bent forward in a rush and kissed her gently on her lips. She leaned into his kiss. Her heart swelled in her chest. She had not been looking for love. But she had found it.

She awoke in her bed in the palace. The dream was gone. Dev was gone. The sky outside the windows was clear and blue again.

"Dev!" she cried. She threw her blankets off of her and rushed through the rooms of her suite.

The main door of her suite slammed against the wall as she threw it open. She raced with bare feet down the hallway and skidded to a stop outside the oversized door to the Guardian's, no- Dev's, own living quarters.

She breathed hard. Her heart raced.

Should she knock? Or push the doors open and go to him?

It would be highly inappropriate for her to enter his suite unaccompanied. Especially in her nightgown.

But she didn't care.

She pushed the doors open. The rooms mirrored her own, but on a larger scale. Where her rooms were bright and welcoming, his were dark. The wood, the furniture. The unlit candles and cold fireplace.

She threw the door to his sleeping chamber open. His massive four post bed was empty. The blankets undisturbed. He had not slept there the previous night.

"Dev!" She yelled. She turned in a frantic circle. She searched every corner and closet in his suite. "Dev!"

She looked out of his window where he had watched her both awake and in her dreams. The garden was still and empty. The sky was clear and bright.

From this vantage point she could see far. Looming over the sky near the end of her line of sight were rain clouds.

She knew deep down inside that he provided rain to her home and lands. He had sacrificed his heart so he could save her people.

She sank to the floor. Her heart ached. It nearly cracked. She had saved her people. But she had lost him.

"I want to be with you," she whispered. She placed her palm flat against the windowpane. The glass felt icy.

When her tears finally dried, she returned to her own rooms. She scooped her bag off the chair beside her bed. She dressed in her original clothes from home, clean of the mud that had stained them before.

She wandered the rooms of the palace with her bag slung across her body. Maybe Dev would return. She lingered as long as she could.

He did not return. Her heart broke into pieces.

She walked out the palace doors.

Instead of a path that led her into the garden, the road to the forest was wide, flat, straight. No askew cobblestones. No ornate iron gate. Not only that, but a ride had been provided to carry her home.

The palace no longer begged her to stay.

Indira's whole body felt numb as she stared at the strange elk-like creature with feathers along its body. It did not have wings, however, and Indira wondered how it would carry her home any better than Mistress Mena's mule.

She approached the magical creature. It stayed still and waited for her to mount.

She hesitated. She looked back at the castle. She needed to go home. But she wanted to stay. To be with Dev.

Tears streamed down her face as she struggled to choose.

Dev's voice whispered in her head. "Go home, Indi. Be free from worry. Find joy."

She turned, hoping he would be there again. He was not.

She yelled at the sky. "But I want to be with you!"

No reply. Nothing. He was truly gone from her.

The strange, feathered elk creature carried her home at such a fast pace that Indira's surroundings were a blur on either side of her. In less than an hour she had been carried down the mountain, across the barren lands, and delivered to her village.

The rain fell for days. She expected flash flooding and damage from the sudden downpour. But just as the gardens and rooms at the palace had a magical quality to them that didn't make sense to her, the rain only brought good things.

The ground turned green within days. The river flowed freely once more. Trees returned to their full-leafed versions overnight.

Flowers bloomed out of season. The dry, dead vegetable gardens sprung to life and new fruits burdened the plants within a week.

The entire village marveled at the sudden change. But no one questioned it. Legends had been told about things like this happening long ago. They accepted it as a miracle and didn't look back.

Indi, though, looked back. Her heart ached for dreams of Dev. Or steely stares from the Guardian version of him. She missed the palace. She missed the maze-like gardens. She missed Dev. Both versions of him.

Her heart remained as cool as the snow on the mountain. Kian, as she had hoped, had already moved on to some other girl from the village now that his father no longer had a chance of absorbing Indira's family business.

To Indira's dismay, Dev did not appear in her dreams no matter how many times she wished for him to be there. No matter how many times she begged with her heart and words for him to come.

When she was awake, she relived all the little moments that should have felt like nothing but had meant everything to her. To them.

Once she was sure that her family was safe, that her village was well-taken care of, Indira rode Mistress Mena's mule northward. The old woman told her that it was of no use. But Indira couldn't believe it. She knew Dev would be there in his ice palace. She couldn't stand the thought of not trying to be with him.

When she attempted to climb the mountain again and return to the palace, she only ended up wandering in circles and finding herself at the base of the mountain again and again. The enchantments that kept most people from finding the Guardian kept her away now, too.

Mistress Mena invited Indi to tell her about her time with the Guardian. Indi told her everything. Except the part about her dreams with Dev. And falling in love with him only to have her heart broken.

When Indi attempted to return the rose pendant, she found the necklace missing from her neck. When had she lost it? She was certain she had worn it when she returned home.

Mistress Mena waved away Indi's apologies. "I'm sure it will turn up eventually," Her smile crinkled the corners of her eyes and mouth.

"A ship from the northlands will be arriving next week," Indira's father told the family at dinner one night about a month after the land had been restored.

"What business do the Northlanders have with us?" Indira's oldest brother asked. He was apprenticing with her father just as she had done when she was younger. As she had thought she wanted to do again. But her dreams were no longer filled with far off adventures and stormy seas.

Why was a ship from the northlands coming? It didn't make any sense. They shipped to the coastlands, but the northlands had their own river systems. They always did their trade at the ports. None had ever ventured upriver to their village before. Indira tried to care but failed. She continued to eat her meal in silence.

"I do not know. The rumor is their prince is touring the land to get a better understanding of their trading associates." Indira's father didn't seem concerned about the visit.

"A prince!" the younger girls squealed with delight. "I wonder if he is handsome?"

"I wonder if he is single," Indira's mother nudged Indira with her elbow and winked.

Indira rolled her eyes. She lowered her head and focused on her meal.

Now that she had experienced affection with Dev, she didn't know if she wanted to try to find love again. What if it only led to more heartbreak? And besides, a prince would not be looking for a wife in their village. Any hope that any of the women had of that was pointless.

"What do we know about him?" another of Indi's brothers asked very diplomatically.

Indira's father explained the rumors he had heard. He was a young man, not heir to his kingdom's throne. He had been away from his home for some time and had recently returned. His mother, the queen, wasn't thrilled about him leaving again so soon to travel, but he had insisted it was necessary.

Indira left the table while her father talked about the Northlander prince. She went to tend to their now thriving garden behind their house. She didn't need to hear about some prince. It only made her thoughts return to her time with Dev.

The following week passed with the town growing more excited about the honored visit. They decorated the streets with banners. Planned an elaborate feast to welcome the prince. And prepared piles of fruit baskets, handmade rugs, clothing, sandals, and even some jewelry that showcased their skills. Indira doubted the prince had any need of any of the gifts, but she understood the people's desire to impress the prince.

She, however, planned to stay home.

The day of the prince's arrival came. Indira's mother and sisters begged her to join them at the docks to welcome the entourage from the northlands. She insisted she wanted some peace and quiet, a commodity not often found in their bustling home.

With great reluctance, the rest of her family left in their finest clothing to greet the prince.

"Finally, some alone time." Indira hadn't realized how much she had missed the quiet palace until the house was empty for the first time since her return.

Only a little bit later, Indira could hear her family

returning up the hill.

"Well, that was fast." She opened the front door to greet them. That's when she saw the whole family plus a whole lot of other people. People definitely not from her village.

The crowd was a contrast of dark features beside light features. The guests had pale skin and hair in various shades from auburn to orange to strawberry blond.

Indira stood in front of the house and gaped at the crowd. So much for a quiet day!

Her mother approached with a wide smile on her face. "He asked to see you specifically," she hissed in Indi's ear.

"What?" She gave her mother a confused look. How could the prince even know about her? It didn't make any sense.

She looked back toward the people gathered in front of her house. A man stepped forward between the others.

"Dev?" she whispered. Was her mind playing tricks on her? Was this a dream?

"Prince Devland of the Northlands is the appropriate way to address His Highness," a red-bearded man spoke with authority.

"Ignore him," Dev announced.

He took three quick steps and stopped a half-step in front of Indira. His familiar smile lit up his whole face.

She couldn't take her eyes off of his shining blue ones. Her stomach was in her throat. Her heart felt like it would beat right out of her chest. Her palms sweated. She felt dizzy.

"What's happening?" she asked in a weak voice.

"I think you forgot something when you left…" He held out Mistress Mena's rose pendant in the palm of his hand.

She didn't know what to think. "Are you… real? Are you really here?" She looked around in a daze.

Dev let out a soft chuckle. "I am really here."

"But, how?"

He leaned close so only she could hear. "When I let you go and sent the rain, it broke the curse. I don't fully understand it myself. But my memories of who I was, where I came from came back to me.

"I had been lost on the mountain. I would have frozen to death if I hadn't been turned into the Mountain Guardian. In a way, the curse saved my life. It also brought me you."

His eyes shone with wonder. And love.

"I returned to my human form. I wanted to come to you at once, but I needed to return home first. To let my mother and my family know I was safe. They were very reluctant to let me leave again after having been gone for so many years, but I finally convinced them."

He gripped both her upper arms beneath his hands. He moved even closer and peered through her eyes right into her soul. Or so it seemed. She still didn't understand.

"I'm here now, Indi. I want to be with you." His hands reached around her neck to clasp the necklace in place. His fingers tickled her skin. It sent a shiver down her spine.

He held each of her upper arms in one of his hands and looked deep into her eyes. "I know you had dreams of sailing the seas. Of not being anyone's 'little wife.' But if you will have me, I promise to never leave you again. I will follow you beyond the horizon on whatever grand adventure you wish."

Tears filled Indira's eyes. She was in shock. She started to sway.

Dev supported her with an arm across her back and helped lower her to sit on a bench on the porch. Light and love danced in his eyes.

"It's real, Indi. I love you." His voice was warm, rough, and sweet.

Realization washed over her from head to toe. She woke up from her stupor. She didn't care that her whole family, and his staff and friends surrounded her. She threw her arms around his neck and sobbed into his shoulder.

He wrapped her in his embrace.

When the sobs slowed, she turned her head and kissed him.

After her tears dried and the kiss had lasted long enough, they pulled apart. He leaned his forehead against hers.

"Well?" he asked her with a wide smile across his face.

"Yes, Dev. Forever yes!"

"It won't ruin your dreams of adventure?" he asked in a serious tone. No sarcasm, teasing, or jokes. He had to be sure.

"Prince Devland of the Northlands…" Indira pressed her forehead against his. She kissed his lips before she continued. "Finding your other half is an adventure. Love is a worthwhile dream."

"Even if I'm not a pirate?" He beamed, looked at her lips, and kissed her again.

"Even if you're just a prince," she teased.

He let out a happy, relieved laugh, picked her up and swung her in a circle, then returned her to her feet.

He cupped her face gently with one hand and gazed into her eyes. When she couldn't hold herself back any longer, she planted both her hands on the side of his face, pulled him toward her, and kissed him. Deep, passionate. Real.

When they broke apart and turned to face the cheering crowd, hand in hand, Indira spotted Mistress Mena at the back of the group. She had a knowing smile on her face. With a simple wave, the woman turned and slowly made her way back down the hill toward her home.

"Thank you," Indira whispered even though she knew the woman could not hear. She gripped the rose pendant in one hand and squeezed Dev's hand with her other.

The
End

Christine Marshall

Welcome to Tala!

All of Christine's fantasy books take place in one fantasy world called **Tala**, pronounced "tall-uh."

Each series or standalone book can be read in any order in relation to the other series or books.

You'll see character crossovers, hidden secrets, and clues to the other stories, characters, and settings as you read the collection. The more you read, the deeper you'll understand Tala and all the characters that live there.

Here's a chronological diagram if you prefer reading in chronological order. Otherwise, pick a book or series that sounds good to you and start there!

Enjoy exploring Tala!

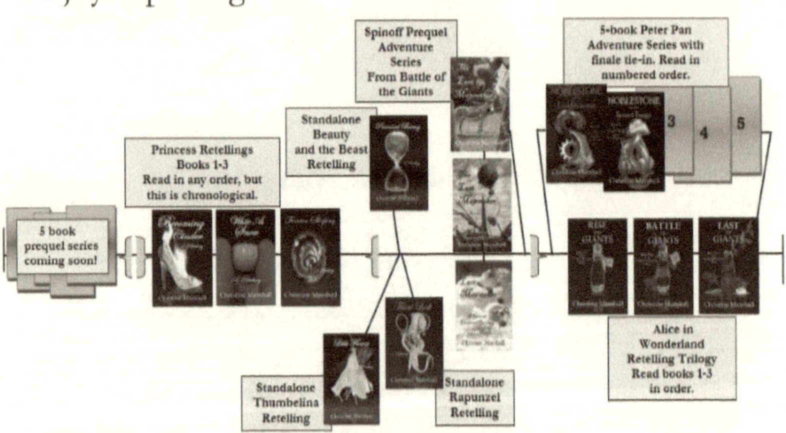

Keep turning pages to learn about each book in the collection (so far!) and don't forget to sign up for Christine's e-newsletter for all the latest news and updates for future books.

Find all Christine's books at CMarshallFantasy Etsy shop and Amazon today.

Buy direct!
CMarshallFantasy
Etsy

Order from
Amazon here

Here's why you'll love these books:

~Mythical creatures like centaurs, griffins, pixies, brownies, elves, golems, giants (of course!), and so many more.

~Magic that prolongs life and heals, and attracts the wrong kind of attention.

~People who can talk to animals and make flowers blossom just by touch.

~Stories of friendship, romance, family connections, and epic journeys that will keep you reading for hours.

What happens to Jessamine next?
Why does Juliette ask Jessamine to come home?
What happened to Peter?
Read the next book in the series from Juliette's
perspective.

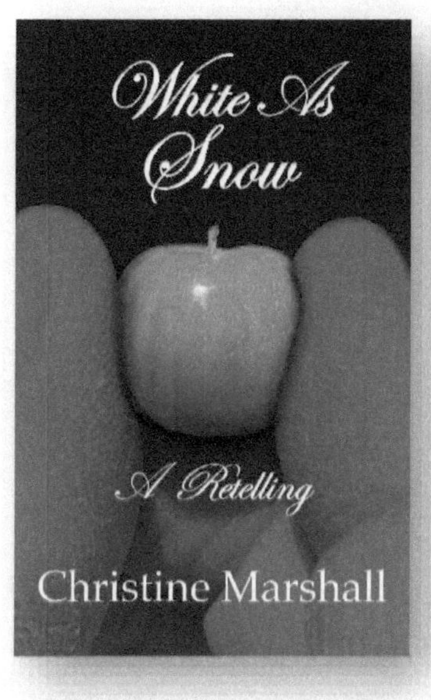

A princess in hiding.
A huntsman as her protector.
Seven unlikely companions by her side.
Can she stop the growing evil threatening her
world?

Add **White As Snow** to your bookshelf now!

Available in print, ebook, and audiobook.

The *Charlie and the Giants* trilogy
inspired by *Alice in Wonderland.*
Book One

Fifteen-year-old Charlie leaves home and ventures into the unknown to battle monsters, befriend fairies and giants, and discover who she really is. Oh, and try to save the world.

Book Two

What happens when the land of wonder is broken upon Charlie's return?

Who will she find this time to help her put an end once and for all to the evil that has spread?

How can a girl full of dreams face the reality of what must be done?

A tale of strange creatures, twists and turns, and ever-growing darkness.

Book Three

The final chapter in an epic saga of fairy tales, princesses, and a world of dreams.

From the Queen of Cinders to the Queen of All.

From a powerless princess to a Princess of power.

From a girl with dreams to a Dreamer destined to save the world.

Christine's *Charlie and the Giants* books are filled with magic, mythical creatures, and an *awesome* female protagonist that has to figure out who she wants to become.

Available in print, ebook, and audiobook.

Get ready for another exciting fantasy adventure!

Steampunk? *Check!*
Pirates? *Check!*
Dwarves? *Check!*
Peter Pan vibes? *Check!*

These books are perfect for readers young and old who love friendship, family, and adventure!

The Last Mapmaker:
A Series of Intentional Disasters
A spinoff humor series

Readers young and old will fall in love with brownie brothers Max and Eliot who have a penchant for mischief as they go on a series of crazy adventures.
These guys will make you laugh and keep you turning pages.

Available in print and ebook.

Join brownie brothers Max and Eliot as they go on another wild adventure, this time into the clouds. Tag along as they encounter cloud dragons, giants, mermaids, and leave a trail of mayhem in their path.
You'll laugh til you cry and then laugh some more.

Available in print and ebook.

Fantasy world? Check!
Playful antics? Check!
Fun for the whole family? Check!
Positive sibling relationships? Check!

Let Max and Eliot take you on another exciting adventure!

The Last Mapmaker Volume 3: A Series of Intentional Disasters (Charlie and the Giants): Marshall, Christine: 9781965310021: Amazon.com: Books
www.amazon.com

CMarshallFantasy Etsy

Also see what kind of trouble these two cause in the **Charlie and the Giants** series where they make their appearance in **Battle of the Giants.**

Available in print and ebook.

Read our Illustrated Guides of Tala!

Insects & Mechanical Things Creatures

Dragons & Flying

Unexpected Creatures

Folk Creatures

Order Here!

Check out Steve Marshall's coloring book with 100 illustrations!

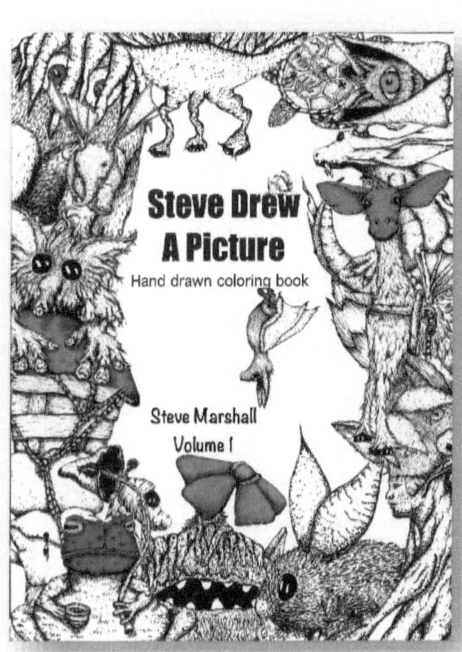

Amazon.com: Steve Drew a Picture: Hand Drawn Coloring Book, Volume 1: Original Illustrations by the Artist to Color for Kids, Teens, Adults: Stress Relief, ... Animals, Mushrooms, Flowers, Dragons, Pixies: 9781965310090: Marshall, Steve, Marshall, Christine: Books

www.amazon.com

Sign up for Christine's e-newsletter!

Check out Christine's website!
www.ChristineMarshallAuthor.com

Christine's Amazon author page:

E&O Creative's Etsy shop
Featuring art by Steve, signed books by Christine,
and other awesome swag!

Coloring books featuring illustrations from Steve
including chapter heading art from Christine's
books!

Acknowledgements

Promised Beauty would not have been possible without a lot of amazing people!

Beta readers: Steve, Belle, Sophie, and Pepper. Y'all rock!

Moral support: Sumedha (my inspiration for Indira!), Shaylen, and Kira Fire- great friends who share their love are the best thing ever!

Original cover art & chapter heading art: my amazing husband, **Steve**, thank you for being my love story inspiration… again! ❤
And thank you for the collaboration on the story and the art. I love you too much.

Other awesome support: Cali, Sarah, Miranda, Jennie, Catie, Ashlee, Joanne, Sherri (& Taco!), Rachel, Tanya, The Fiberista, A. Perdue, Abbie, Samantha, Cindy's 5th grade class, Sarah's English teacher, and so many more- thank you for continuing to share my books and support us in our publishing journey! We are blessed to know you all!!

To everyone who has read, promoted, and reviewed my books, thank you! I never imagined social media would be such a community for a reader and author like me.

About the Author

When Christine isn't spinning tales on her laptop, she probably has a book and a chocolate chip cookie in hand. She loves all kinds of books: fantasy, sci-fi, historical fiction, non-fiction, and even textbooks.

She also loves to play her ukulele, stand in the rain, stay up late, and try new foods... but not all at the same time! Christine has moved over 20 times in the past 20 years, and firmly believes that people are more important than things.

Photo Credit: Amber Richards